"Why does Garth let you stay in the villa when you're so rude?"

Jack shrugged and threw himself down on one of the wicker chairs. "Let's just say that Garth and I have…an understanding. We use each other, but we have as little to do with each other as possible."

When Callie looked at him over her shoulder suspiciously, Jack was grinning, blue eyes glinting wickedly. His smile confused her and she turned quickly back to the sea. She didn't know what to make of Jack Kingsley. She felt that she ought to dislike and distrust him. She did dislike and distrust him—but there was something in his smile and the dancing humor in his eyes….

D0561394

Jessica Hart had a haphazard career before she began writing to finance a degree in history. Her experience ranged from waitress, theater production assistant and outback cook to news-desk secretary, and she has worked in countries as diverse as France and Indonesia. She now lives in the north of England, where her hobbies are limited to eating well and traveling when she can—preferably to places where she'll find good food or desert or tropical rain.

POSEIDON'S DAUGHTER
Jessica Hart

Harlequin Books

TORONTO • NEW YORK • LONDON
AMSTERDAM • PARIS • SYDNEY • HAMBURG
STOCKHOLM • ATHENS • TOKYO • MILAN
MADRID • WARSAW • BUDAPEST • AUCKLAND

Original hardcover edition published in 1992
by Mills & Boon Limited

ISBN 0-373-17156-0

Harlequin Romance first edition October 1992

POSEIDON'S DAUGHTER

CHAPTER ONE

DROPPING her bags on to the quayside, Callie took off her straw hat and ran her fingers through straight dark hair as she looked about her.

It had taken two flights, a bumpy taxi ride across Ilonika and a ferry to bring her to the tiny island of Pikos, a steep, rocky outcrop set in the Ionian sea, and already the damp greyness of the London spring she had left behind seemed impossibly remote. The little port was sheltered between two pine-covered headlands that curved out into the bay like encircling arms. Whitewashed houses clustered around the shady square and clung to the hillside, their stark design softened by scrambling bougainvillaea, vivid trails of pink and purple, and the bright splashes of geraniums down the steps.

Behind Callie, the ferry had turned around with remarkable speed and was already steaming back around the headland, leaving a couple of fishing boats rocking gently in its wake. It was very quiet. The sea glittered in the intense Greek light and the scent of the pines mingled with salt and dust and sunshine in the fragrant air.

Callie's heart lifted. It was perfect.

The summer stretched ahead of her enticingly. Three months to do the illustrations. Three months to read and swim and explore. Three months on her own.

It had been Antonia's idea, of course. Antonia, who had never liked Neil and felt guilty about Stefan. 'Why just go for two weeks?' she had asked when Callie had come home starry-eyed at having won her first big commission to illustrate a book of Greek myths for children and had announced her intention of going to Greece for inspiration.

'I can't really afford to go for any longer,' Callie said, calculating how much she could save from her waitressing wages on the back of an envelope. 'Three weeks at a push, but I'd have to skimp on that.'

'Is Neil going with you?' Antonia asked, too casually.

'No.' Callie kept her head bent over her envelope.

'He's been so attentive recently that I'm surprised he's letting you go off on your own. I thought you were getting back together again.'

Callie sighed. 'That's what Neil thinks too. He's assumed that we can just carry on as we were before I met Stefan.'

'And you don't want to do that?'

'It's not that I don't want to, it's just that I can't be like Neil and pretend that nothing happened.' She sat back in her chair and twisted the pen absently between her hands. 'Sometimes I wish I could. I've known Neil for five years, and I suppose I'm used to having him around, but I know that if I went back to him now I'd just be using him. Going to Greece alone is a way of proving to him—and to myself—that I can manage on my own.'

'Good!' Antonia nodded with satisfaction. 'I've always thought you'd be better off without Neil, Callie. He's so pompous and smug, and he's taken you for granted for years! I have to admit that I was delighted when you fell for Stefan, but if I'd known how badly he would hurt you I'd never have introduced you.' She glanced at her friend's averted face. 'I do feel guilty about Stefan, Callie. I should have known what he was like.'

Callie swallowed. Falling in and out of love with Stefan had been such a humiliating experience that she still found it hard to talk about it. 'It wasn't your fault. I learnt my lesson with Stefan, and, if nothing else, it proved that I didn't really love Neil. If you hadn't introduced me to Stefan, Neil and I would still be plodding on in the old routine. As it is, I've decided to make a real break from everything, and this commission is the ideal opportunity to do that.'

'If you want a proper break, you'll need longer than two or three weeks,' said Antonia, whose face had cleared with relief at Callie's determinedly sensible attitude. She prowled over to the window and stood staring out at the rain, deep in thought.

A silence fell. Callie stared down at the sums on the envelope and thought about Neil. Sometimes she despaired of making him understand that she couldn't go back to being the meek, biddable girl he had got used to having around.

Suddenly Antonia swung around. 'If I could arrange free accommodation for you, that would leave you enough to live on for the summer, wouldn't it?'

'Yes,' Callie said cautiously, glancing at her figures again. 'I've already set aside enough for the flight, and if I didn't have to pay for rooms I'm sure the rest would cover food...' She stared at Antonia. 'I didn't know you knew anyone in Greece. How would you be able to arrange it?'

'Well...' Antonia leant forward confidentially. 'You know Garth Havelock?'

Callie didn't even bother to nod, although her eyes widened. Of course she knew of Garth Havelock. Most people did. After taking the literary world by storm with his first novel, Garth had walked off with numerous prizes and awards in spite of his well-known aversion to publicity. He refused interviews, disdained chat shows, and had gradually acquired a reputation as a brilliant, temperamental recluse whose very inaccessibility promoted a fever of speculative interest. Callie was one of his greatest fans. She read his novels again and again, and was very impressed that Antonia, who worked in a very lowly capacity for his agent, Stella, sometimes actually spoke to him on the phone. Antonia was less overwhelmed by this extraordinary honour, but then Antonia's literary tastes were not exactly highbrow, and she could be disconcertingly unromantic and down-to-earth at times.

'Garth has got a villa on some Greek island,' Antonia was saying. 'It's not very exciting—no beaches, no bars, no tourists or anything—but you like quiet places, don't you?' she added kindly, and obviously uncomprehendingly. 'Stella goes to stay there sometimes when he's away, so we've got a key at the office. I'm sure you could stay there. Garth's gone to Los Angeles for the summer to work on the screenplay for *The Ninth Labour*, so he'd probably be glad of someone to look after the villa. It's the perfect solution, Callie! I can't think why I didn't think of it straight away.'

Callie hesitated, torn between reluctance to invade her idol's privacy and rising excitement. Garth Havelock's villa! The two weeks she had planned for herself in Greece would have been wonderful, but the thought of a whole summer was almost too good to be true. She could concentrate on the illustrations, put Stefan firmly behind her, and Neil would realise that she meant what she said. Their relationship had dragged on too long, and now it was over.

'There's no harm in asking, is there?' Antonia said persuasively, and Callie succumbed.

'He could always say no,' she said.

But Garth Havelock had not said no. Antonia had come back from the office a few days later, waving a key. 'It's all fixed. Garth Havelock's villa is yours for the summer! All you have to do is get there.'

And now here she was.

Antonia had not exaggerated when she said that Pikos would be very small and very quiet. An old woman, dressed entirely in black, with a stern, seamed face, had been the only other passenger getting off the ferry here, and she had walked stiffly up some crumbling steps and disappeared, leaving Callie alone on the quayside, except for a black and white cat who watched her unblinkingly from a dim doorway.

Callie looked about her a little doubtfully. Which was the Villa Oleander? Antonia had merely said, when she had asked for directions, that it would be silly to bother Garth about details, and, anyway, it was such a tiny place that someone would be bound to be able to direct her.

Jamming her hat back on her head, Callie picked up her bags once more and headed for the square, where a huge cypress cast welcome shade. Four old men sat on straight-backed chairs outside a dim, dark shop, and watched Callie's approach much as the cat had done, their craggy faces and dark, sunken eyes inscrutable.

A comfortably plump woman in an apron was gossiping in the doorway of the taverna with a young girl. Deciding that they looked more approachable than the old men, Callie headed in their direction.

'Excuse me,' she began nervously, wishing that in the flurry of arrangements before she had left she had found time to learn some Greek. 'Could you tell me how to get to the Villa Oleander?'

She was met by a spate of smiling Greek, and bit her lip helplessly. 'Do you speak English?' she tried, without much hope.

More Greek. Suppressing a sigh, Callie pulled out her Greek phrase-book. Getting off the beaten track was all very romantic, she reflected as she thumbed through the pages, but there were disadvantages. Ah, here it was. *'Milate anglika?'* she read out laboriously.

This time the woman beamed, and pointed behind Callie, who turned. A man was sitting at one of the tables that were set out beneath a wicker shade at the water's edge.

At the woman's call, he pushed back his chair and sauntered over. Dressed in faded shorts and T-shirt, he had an aggressively physical presence, and the latent power in the strong brown body was unmistakable. As he got closer she saw that he had intensely dark features and an air of infuriatingly cool self-assurance that reminded her bitterly of Stefan. It was the first time Callie could remember disliking anyone on sight.

The woman gestured towards Callie, talking in rapid Greek, and he replied in the same language, making her laugh. That easy amusement at her expense was like Stefan, too, and Callie stiffened.

As the man glanced at her, one eyebrow raised, she said awkwardly, 'I don't know if you can help? This lady doesn't seem to speak any English.'

'Surely it's a case of your not speaking Greek,' he pointed out, and Callie's jaw dropped.

'You're English!' she said stupidly, and found herself looking into a pair of mocking blue eyes, not a pale, Anglo-Saxon blue, but the deep intense blue of the Mediterranean. Only his voice was undeniably English.

'Why the surprise? Haven't you ever met an Englishman before?'

Callie flushed at the teasing note in his voice. 'It's just . . . I wasn't expecting . . .' she said weakly, adding on a faintly accusing note, 'You don't *look* English.'

The blue eyes inspected her with some amusement, taking in the deceptively fragile-looking slenderness, the pale, pointed, elfin face dominated by a pair of huge silver-grey eyes and framed by obstinately straight black hair. In her loose blue cotton dress and hat, and with her hair tucked behind her ears, she looked much younger than her twenty-four years.

'If it comes to that,' the man said, 'nor do you.'

Under his knowing gaze, Callie was acutely conscious of how crumpled and unsophisticated she must look, and her hand went to check that her hair was still firmly in place away from her face in a gesture that was as unconsciously defensive as it was unnecessary. The hot blue eyes made her uncomfortable.

'Did you want to order a drink? You look hot.' His grin told her that he was well aware of the disturbing effect of his eyes, and that her flush had little to do with the heat.

'No,' Callie said sharply, anxious to get away from him as soon as possible. 'I just wanted to ask the way to the Villa Oleander.'

His smile stilled. The dark brows rose, then snapped into a frown. 'The Villa *Oleander*?'

Mystified by his reaction, Callie nodded. 'Do you know it?'

'I do indeed,' he said slowly. 'Might one ask who you are?'

Callie lifted her chin. 'Might one ask why it's any concern of yours?' she retorted.

A gleam of amusement sprang back into his eyes. 'Merely that I happen to be staying at the Villa Oleander myself!'

'*What?*' Callie exclaimed, aghast. 'You can't be!'

'You're just as much a delightful surprise to me,' he pointed out drily.

'But I thought the villa would be empty!'

His eyes narrowed very slightly. 'Who told you that?'

'Garth Havelock,' Callie said bravely. It was almost the truth. He had told Antonia and Antonia had told her.

'Garth Havelock said you could stay in the villa?' His disbelief was so obvious that Callie's remarkable silvery grey eyes brightened with indignation.

'Yes, he did! I wouldn't dream of being here otherwise! He needed someone to keep an eye on the villa while he's in America, so I just assumed there wouldn't be anyone else here.' Callie fingered the key in her pocket like a talisman. Antonia had assured her that Garth Havelock was delighted at the idea.

'Well, well.' The man was looking at her speculatively and Callie was sure that he was quite unconvinced. 'Good old Garth,' he murmured.

Callie hesitated. 'Are you a friend of his?' she asked at last, and he gave an odd little smile.

'Sort of.'

Which might mean anything, Callie reflected dubiously. If he was a friend, he obviously had a prior claim on the villa, but why then had Garth given permission for her to have the key? Perhaps he had forgotten all about her and made a separate arrangement with this man, whoever he was...

'My name's Jack Kingsley,' he said, answering her unspoken question, and stuck out his hand.

She took it reluctantly. His overt physicality made her nervous, and as his fingers closed over hers, warm and strong, she felt her spine shiver in instinctive reaction.

'Callie Grey,' she muttered.

'Well, Callie Grey, perhaps we'd better sit down and sort this out.'

He pulled out a chair for her at a nearby table, and shouted something in the direction of the taverna. There was a faint answering cry as he sat down opposite her and leant his folded arms on the red plastic tablecloth.

Callie eyed him warily. There was something vaguely disreputable about his dark good looks.

There were the slight pouches beneath his eyes which she always associated with reckless living, and the stubble on his chin added to the impression of daredevil charm. In an earlier age he would have been a pirate or a highwayman or a smuggler, she thought, unsure of whether she was more fascinated or alarmed. His navy-blue eyes held challenge and mockery, and his mouth was long and mobile, quirking at the corners as if permanently amused.

In fact, when she looked carefully, he wasn't as handsome as she had first imagined. His nose was a bit too large, his jaw a bit too square, and, although his thick dark hair had obviously once been well cut, it had long grown out and was now rather shaggy, curling slightly forward below his ears.

She guessed him to be in his late thirties, but it was hard to tell. He was deeply tanned, and he radiated an aggressively masculine confidence that made Callie shift uneasily.

She was a sensitive girl, dreamy, artistic and a little shy, and had always found it hard to cope with boisterously physical people like Jack Kingsley. Neil was an intellectual and Stefan languidly sophisticated, and, in spite of her determination to spend a summer by herself, at that moment Callie would have been glad to see either of them—yes, even Stefan—as protection against the danger she saw dancing in Jack's blue eyes.

'What's Callie short for?' he asked casually, watching the play of emotions on her transparent face.

Callie was unprepared for the question. 'Nothing,' she said, conscious of the tell-tale heat staining her cheeks. Her ridiculous name had been a constant source of embarrassment to her since she was a child, and it would be long before she forgot how cruelly mocking Stefan had been when she had given in and told him.

'It must be short for something,' Jack protested. 'Come on, you can tell me! Caroline? Camilla? Carol?'

'No.'

'Calpurnia? Calandra? Clarissa? Crystal?'

'Of course not!' It was much worse, if only he knew!

'What, then?'

'It's none of your business,' Callie said defensively, feeling as if she were being pushed back against her chair by the sheer force of his personality.

Jack's dark blue eyes crinkled at the corners when he smiled. 'You might as well tell me. I'll find out in the end.'

'Shall we discuss the villa?' she suggested through gritted teeth.

'Ah, yes, you were telling me some story about Garth wanting a housekeeper.'

'It's not a story!' Callie pulled the key Antonia had given her out of her pocket. 'Look, here's the key to the villa.'

Jack took it and turned it thoughtfully between his fingers, frowning slightly. 'It's the key to the Villa Oleander all right.' He rubbed his thumb along the teeth of the key and then, lifting his head, inspected her with eyes that had sharpened suddenly to a direct, penetrating blue. 'Tell me, how exactly do you know Garth?'

There was a tiny pause. Callie was unwilling to admit that she only knew the famous writer through his work. 'A friend of mine is his agent's secretary,' she said cautiously.

'Ah . . . Antonia?'

'Yes.' She looked at him, startled and insensibly reassured. 'Do you know her?'

'I know of her.' He handed back the key. 'It all begins to make sense.'

'What does?'

'Your arrival.' He broke off as the girl from the taverna appeared with a tray, which she set down carefully. She placed two smudgy glasses on the table, together with a carafe of water.

'*Efharisto, Katerina.*' Jack smiled up at the girl with his thanks. He had an extraordinarily attractive, slightly lop-sided smile that emphasised the laughter lines about his eyes and deepened the crease in one cheek.

His teeth were white and very even, Callie noticed before she looked determinedly away. Stefan had

had a nice smile too, and look where *that* had got her!

'*Parakalo.*' Katerina smiled back down at him, obviously not immune to its effect either. She cast a curious, half-envious glance at Callie as she picked up the tray and made her way back to the taverna.

Jack sloshed some water from the carafe into the glasses, turning the liquid cloudy, and pushed one across to Callie. 'Have some ouzo.'

Callie sniffed at her glass a little dubiously. She had never tasted ouzo before, and hadn't expected it to smell quite like that. About to put the glass back down, she glanced up and caught Jack watching her. He was tilting back in his chair, interpreting her expression without difficulty, and his eyes were alight with amusement. He wasn't actually smiling, but the crease in his cheek was very pronounced.

What was so funny? Callie thought crossly, changing her mind and taking a defiant gulp of the ouzo. It took all her self-control not to grimace at the taste as she replaced the glass carefully on the table and met Jack's gaze, challenge in her grey eyes. Sunlight through the wicker dappled her skin and gave her a fey, elusive look at odds with her obvious struggle to control her expression.

'*Is iyian*!' he toasted her mockingly. 'Cheers!' Tossing back his ouzo in one go, he let his chair crash back to the ground and leant across the table towards Callie, who recoiled instinctively. His closeness made her nervous: he was too vibrant, too physical, too everything.

'So,' said Jack, 'what exactly are you doing here?'

'I've told you. I've come to look after the villa while Mr Havelock's away.'

'I don't want you to think that I don't believe you, but Garth Havelock is frequently away, and he's never needed anyone to look after the villa before.'

Callie studied her glass and wished the line of Jack's mouth wouldn't keep dancing in front of her eyes. 'No, well, I think he was just being kind.'

'Kind? Garth?' Jack gave a shout of laughter and then shook his head incredulously. 'That's a new one on me!'

Offended by his implied criticism of her hero, Callie's mouth tightened angrily. 'I don't suppose for a minute that he really needs a housekeeper. But he knows that I can't afford to stay in Greece for the summer otherwise, and I think he's letting me look after the house as a way of not accepting any rent. I call that kind!'

Jack looked at her curiously. 'And why are you so dependent on Garth's *kindness*?'

'I'm an illustrator, or at least I'm trying to be. I've been scraping by doing odd jobs, mostly wait-ressing, to keep myself going while I tried to make a name for myself.' She was turning the glass be-tween her hands, remembering the years of drudgery to pay her rent, the endless touting round of her portfolio, the odd jobs to keep her hope alive, but when she lifted her head to look at Jack her eyes were luminous, bright with remembered excitement. 'A few weeks ago I got my first big commission. They want me to illustrate a children's book of Greek myths, but I have to have the illustrations ready by September. If I'd stayed in London I'd have had to carry on waitressing just to keep a roof over my head. Here, I can concentrate on the drawings.'

Her gaze slid past Jack to the bay. The rocky shoreline, the sunlight flashing on the sea, the scent of pines in the clean air, all had a still, timeless quality. The ancient Greeks would have looked out at much the same view, she reflected, half expecting to see Odysseus to come sailing round the headland.

'So where does Garth Havelock come into all this?' Jack Kingsley's prosaic voice brought her back to the present.

Callie hesitated. To tell the truth, she wasn't at all sure how Antonia had broached the subject with Garth. She had been too elated at the prospect of a summer in Greece to ask too many questions.

'Antonia knew he was going to be in Los Angeles all summer, and she asked him if I could come here while he was away. I think she must have explained that I didn't have much money, because Garth said that I could stay here for free, in exchange for keeping an eye on the villa.'

She could still remember the rush of relief and excitement on hearing that Garth had agreed, followed almost immediately by shamefaced panic at how she would cope on her own. It was all very well making grand plans, but she was used to Neil dealing with everything, and in spite of all she had said to Antonia she wasn't at all sure she would manage by herself. Neil's reaction had been predictably one of pained surprise when she had told him. She was far too dreamy and impractical to get herself to Greece, far less spend a whole summer there, he had told her; there was no need for her to spend all her savings; if she would just wait until he had finished his thesis, he would take her to the Edinburgh Festival.

In the past Callie had always agreed with Neil's suggestions. He was so much more capable and intelligent than she was that it had been easier to let him do all the organising, but her disastrous experience with Stefan had left her with a harder shell about her emotions. Encouraged by Antonia, she had insisted. She didn't want to go to Edinburgh. She wanted to go to Greece.

Not that she had any intention of explaining all that to Jack Kingsley. 'It was too good a chance to turn down,' was all she said. 'So I handed in my notice at the restaurant, found someone to share the flat with Antonia and, well, here I am.' Her smile went a little awry. 'It was the most adventurous thing I'd ever done. It never occurred to me that there would be anyone else here...'

Was that a note of self-pity creeping into her voice? Callie caught herself up sternly and tried, not very successfully, to sound brisk. 'Anyway, it can't be helped. I'll just have to make other plans.'

She stared back out to sea, contemplating the dismal prospect of going back to London after a couple of weeks. Neil wouldn't be at all surprised. Suddenly she felt very tired and vulnerable. There had been so many last-minute details to sort out before she had left that she felt as if she had been running around in circles for weeks, and Neil's refusal to believe that she meant what she said had not made things any easier. Callie's silver-grey eyes shadowed. If she went home so soon, all that effort would be wasted...

Jack had been watching her, but now he sat back in his chair. 'I don't see that there's an insuperable problem,' he said abruptly. 'The villa's big enough for two. No reason why we shouldn't both stay there.'

'You mean *share*?'

He grinned at her astonished expression. 'Is it such an extraordinary idea?'

'But...I don't know you.'

'I don't know you either, but we both know Antonia...and Garth, of course.'

Callie's long dark lashes swept down over her eyes, unwilling to meet that sharp blue stare. She'd already implied that she knew Garth, so she could hardly admit now that she had never met him. After all, Jack had only claimed to be a 'sort of' friend.

He probably didn't know Garth any better than she did.

'You haven't much choice, anyway,' Jack went on when she didn't speak. 'There won't be another ferry until next week.'

'Surely there are some rooms to let on the island?' Callie said, feeling that the situation was changing a little too fast for her. Neil would have known what to do immediately.

'One or two maybe, but Pikos is off the tourist route, and it doesn't really cater for visitors. They won't be cheap.'

'Oh.' Callie sipped uncertainly at her ouzo. A week of expensive accommodation would ruin her budget, and even if she moved somewhere cheaper when the next ferry came she would only be able to stretch to another week or so at the most. It was nice of Jack to suggest that she stay at the villa ... although she could swear that he was not the kind of man to do anything unless it suited him. It was hard to see what he would get out of having an unwanted guest around, though. Perhaps he was leaving soon anyway?

'How long will you be staying at the villa?' she asked hopefully.

'That depends,' said Jack unhelpfully as his eyes, blue and amused, travelled lazily over her.

Callie bit her lip. 'Wouldn't I disturb you?'

'Oh, I don't think so.' His swift smile was sheer devilry, quickening her pulse alarmingly and setting her heart thumping in nervous response. 'Not in the way you mean, anyway!'

Thrown off balance by her reaction, Callie took another gulp from her glass and tried to think sensibly about her situation.

She didn't know anything about Jack Kingsley. Every instinct warned her against him. He was a dangerously attractive man, but she had learnt her lesson about dangerously attractive men, hadn't she? Once bitten, twice shy.

But at least he knew Antonia. That was something. Not much, but something. It might be a bit awkward sharing a house with a stranger, but it shouldn't be too difficult to keep out of his way. Jack was right: what choice did she have, really? Her only alternative was to go home after two or three weeks, but it would mean finding another job and somewhere else to live now that Antonia had let her room for the summer. And then there was Neil...

'All right.' Callie made up her mind. She looked straight at Jack, grey eyes direct beneath her fringe. 'I'll stay.' And then, as an afterthought, 'Thank you.'

CHAPTER TWO

JACK waved a casual hand. 'Don't thank me, thank Garth.'

'Oh, I will,' Callie said fervently.

'Funny old bird, isn't he?' Jack sat back in his chair, crossed one leg to rest his ankle on the other knee and watched her intently.

Old? Callie had no idea how old Garth Havelock was, but she had somehow assumed that he was quite young. Jack's comment was deliberately provocative, she was sure, but she was determined not to rise to the bait. He couldn't possibly know that she had never met Garth.

'I think he's generous, sensitive and a marvellous writer,' she said, avoiding a direct answer.

'Really?' Jack tipped back his head and gazed at the wicker shade. There was a suggestion of a smile about his mouth. 'I'd have said forgetful, selfish and pretentious was a better description.'

Callie stared at him, gratitude forgotten at his casual criticism of Garth. 'How can you say that?' she demanded, outraged.

'Well, clearly I know him better than you do, if you're so surprised!' Jack grinned appreciatively across the table at her hostile face. 'How long have you known him?'

'Not very long,' Callie said cautiously. She hadn't met him in the flesh, but she was convinced that she knew him well through his writing. His warmth and compassion, his intelligence and sensitivity shone clearly in his novels. Few writers managed to combine popular success with such critical acclaim. 'Perhaps you do know him better than I,' she said, tilting her chin in a characteristic gesture, 'but it would take more than *your* say-so to change my opinion of him!'

'Does Garth know he's got such a loyal champion?' Jack teased, obviously highly amused, and Callie, normally the gentlest of souls, longed to hit him.

'Does he know he's got such an ungrateful "sort-of" friend?' she retorted.

Jack's smile only broadened. 'Oh, yes,' he said. 'He knows me just as well as I know him.' He reached over and appropriated Callie's glass. 'I'll have that if you're not going to drink it. No point in wasting it.' Draining it in one go, he set the glass down with a click on the plastic tablecloth. 'Ready?'

Callie looked blankly at him.

'I presume you'd like to see the villa?' he said patiently. 'You look tired.'

'Oh, yes . . . yes.' She got to her feet, stumbling slightly as exhaustion overwhelmed her suddenly. Her flight had arrived in Athens at three that morning, so she had hardly slept at all, but it had

taken Jack's comment to make her realise quite how
tired she was.

'Are you OK?' Jack asked, reaching out to steady
her.

Callie nodded, disconcerted as much by the
concern in his eyes as by the energy and vitality she
felt surging through her at his impersonal touch.
She was glad when he dropped his hand and bent
to pick up her bags, ignoring her protests.

It was just as well Jack was so obnoxious about
Garth Havelock, she reflected as she trudged
wearily beside him. It would make it so much easier
to ignore just how attractive he could be.

The Villa Oleander stood at the end of a dusty track
that wound through olive groves, about a mile from
the port. Perched on the edge of a steep hillside, it
seemed from the back a deceptively low whitewashed building, surrounded by great clumps of
pink oleanders that gave it its name, but inside it
was far bigger than Callie had imagined.

Wide-eyed, she walked down an open-tread
staircase from the bedrooms at ground-floor level
to a vast living area, furnished simply, but dra-
matically, in blue and white and dark wood. An
enormous window ran the length of the room.

'Like it?' asked Jack as Callie slid open the door
leading on to a terrace cluttered with pots of geraniums and petunias and daisies. Shaded by a vine-
laden pergola, it jutted out over the sea, and steps
cut into the rock led down to a small jetty.

'Like it?' Callie repeated, lifting her hands and then dropping them helplessly, unable to find adequate words. 'It's wonderful!' Her smile illuminated her face, transforming the rather serious, sprite-like expression into sudden radiance.

Dreamily unaware of the suddenly arrested look in Jack's eyes, she wandered over to lean on the terrace wall and peer down at the sea lapping gently against the rocks below. In the fading light, it had deepened to just the colour of Jack's eyes.

She straightened abruptly at the thought. 'Imagine wanting to spend the summer in a city when you could be here!' she said to fill the sudden silence.

'In a city?' Jack sounded puzzled.

'I thought Garth was in Los Angeles?'

'Oh, yes . . . well, I told you, he's an odd sort of bloke.'

Callie frowned. 'I can't imagine why he lets you stay here when you're so rude about him,' she said crossly.

Jack shrugged and threw himself down on one of the wicker chairs. He stuck his feet on the table. 'Let's just say that Garth and I have . . . an understanding. We use each other, but we have as little to do with each other as possible.'

He made Garth Havelock sound somewhat sinister, but when Callie looked at him over her shoulder suspiciously he was grinning, blue eyes glinting wickedly. His smile confused her and she turned quickly back to the sea. She didn't know

what to make of Jack Kingsley. She felt that she
ought to dislike and distrust him, she *did* dislike
and distrust him, but there was something in his
smile and the dancing humour in his eyes which
tugged at her all the same. And she would have to
share the villa with him, so she might as well make
an effort to be pleasant...

'What do you do?' she asked, turning round to
lean back against the wall.

'Do?' Jack settled himself more comfortably in
the chair. 'This and that. A bit of fishing, a bit of
swimming. Quite a bit of sitting here with a beer
and admiring the view.'

'I meant when you're not on holiday,' Callie said,
a little frostily. He must have known perfectly well
what she meant.

'Who said I was on holiday?'

'I presume you don't live like this the whole time!
Don't you work?'

'As little as possible. What's the point in working
when you could spend the summer here instead?'

'Or when it's so much easier to take advantage
of Garth Havelock's generosity?' Callie suggested
with an edge of sarcasm.

'Exactly!' Jack beamed at her. 'I can see that
you understand. After all, you're in the same position, aren't you?'

'At least I don't make a profession of it!' she
said, but her grey eyes slid away from Jack's face
and dull colour crept up her throat. She *was* taking

advantage of Garth, just as she had accused Jack of doing.

'I shouldn't worry about it,' said Jack comfortably. 'Garth doesn't mind.'

'How can you know that?' Callie's face was serious as she picked a dead head off a geranium, unwilling to look directly at Jack. 'He must get awfully sick of people sponging off him just because he's rich and successful.'

'Oh, I don't know. I think it depends on the people. Why on earth should he object to a beautiful girl like you staying here?'

Beautiful? Callie's head jerked up, amazed at Jack's description. She had never considered herself beautiful: she was too small, her horrible hair was too dark and lank, her face was too pointed, her mouth too wide.

'You *are* rather beautiful, you know,' Jack said, reading her expression, his eyes crinkling with amusement. 'In an ethereal, unusual sort of way. Hasn't anybody ever told you so?'

Callie shook her head dumbly, wishing she were the sophisticated sort of girl who knew how to respond to compliments without blushing and stammering and making it sound as if she believed every word. Jack was probably just teasing her.

In the end she cleared her throat and decided to ignore it altogether.

'I'd hate it if Garth thought I was just a silly fan.'

'I thought you *were* a fan of his?'

'I am, but I'm not silly,' Callie said with a touch of hauteur.

'Well, Garth knows you, so he must know that.'

Callie carefully removed another dead geranium and began shredding it with her fingers. 'He doesn't,' she confessed at last, watching the faded red petals drift to the tiles around her feet. 'I've never met Garth Havelock.'

There, it was said. Glancing up shyly from beneath her lashes, she saw that Jack was smiling.

'I didn't think you had.'

'How did you know?' Callie asked, mortified.

'You admire him too much. I can't help feeling that if you'd actually met Garth you wouldn't be quite so impressed.'

'I'm sure I would.' She lifted her chin. 'Nothing would convince me that he's not absolutely wonderful.' She turned her head to look at the rocky headland curving round the little bay, her eyes dreamy. 'I suppose I've always imagined him as my perfect hero, intelligent and witty, but sensitive and compassionate as well. It doesn't matter that I don't know what he looks like. His writing tells me all I want to know.'

Jack was watching her abstracted profile with a curious expression. 'Would you like to meet him?' he asked.

'I'm not sure.' Callie's gaze rested on a clump of yellow broom clinging precariously to the steep cliffs. 'Part of me would love to meet him, but I'd probably be tongue-tied with embarrassment and then he'd think I *was* silly.'

'I don't think he would,' Jack said quietly.

'Anyway, it's probably better to keep him as a dream,' Callie said, as if she hadn't heard him. 'Dream men can sometimes be a bit disappointing in reality,' she added half to herself with a sigh, thinking of Stefan, and surprising an odd flash in Jack's eyes as she turned back to him.

But he said only, 'Perhaps you're right. Garth's a pretty ordinary bloke, really. He nearly had his head turned by all the fuss at the beginning, but too much media attention can swallow you up, and before you know where you are you spend so much time being a personality that you don't have any left to write.' Swinging his legs off the table, Jack leant forward and rested his elbows on his knees. 'Garth made a wise decision to keep himself to himself just in time. No interviews, no chat shows, no book-signing sessions, no reaction to all the nonsense written about his books. Now he just carries on with his life the way he wants to, not the way the PR people want him to.'

'You sound as if you almost admire him,' Callie said in surprise.

'Do I?' That reckless grin again.

'I thought you didn't like him?'

'Oh, I wouldn't go that far. Sometimes I'm really quite fond of him.'

Callie puzzled over Jack's attitude to Garth Havelock as she got ready for bed. He had offered

to take her back down to the taverna for something
to eat, but she was so tired by then that she had
shaken her head and opted for an early night.
Whistling, Jack had disappeared down the dusty
track, and Callie was left alone with her thoughts.

The villa seemed silent and empty without him.
She wished she knew who Jack Kingsley was, and
what exactly his connection with Garth Havelock
was. They seemed an unlikely pair, Garth sensitive
and cultured, Jack so vibrantly physical with that
undercurrent of reckless danger. Even lounging in
the chair with his feet stuck casually up on the table,
he had managed to give the impression of being
ready to spring into action at the flick of a switch.

It occurred to Callie that she had managed to tell
Jack an awful lot about herself since they had met,
without her learning anything at all about him. Not
that she was particularly interested, she assured
herself as she switched off the bathroom light. She
was only concerned on Garth Havelock's account.
She couldn't help feeling that there was more to
Jack's presence at the Villa Oleander than met the
eye, and she wondered if Garth knew any more
about it than she did.

In spite of her exhaustion, Callie slept fitfully,
falling deeply asleep and then waking at unaccustomed noises. She heard Jack come back from the
taverna, still whistling until he obviously remembered she was there, and much later, in the deep,
dark hours of the night, she surfaced at the unmistakable sound of a door being closed carefully

and lowered voices. A little later a boat's engine puttered out into the bay and, groggy with sleep, she turned over, thinking only that it seemed an odd time to go fishing.

When Callie woke properly the next morning the bright sunlight was slanting through the shutters. She lay for a while, watching the stripes of gold on the rough white wall and trying to remember where she was. It was very quiet, but the soft slurp of the sea against the rocks gradually permeated her consciousness and, when somewhere in the distant olive groves a donkey brayed, memory came back with a rush.

She was in Greece! Callie rolled on to her back and stretched with contentment. Today she would re-read all the myths she had loved so much as a child and let their magic work on her again. On an island like this, that would be all the inspiration she would need to start preliminary sketches.

She ought to write to her parents, too, to let them know where she was. How her father would love it here! And Antonia would want to know that she had arrived safely.

Should she write to Neil? Waiting for the connecting flight in Athens yesterday, tired and apprehensive at being alone in a strange country for the first time, she had begun to wonder if he might have been right after all, and she had been overcome with a wave of nostalgia for the nice, safe days when Neil had ordered her life. The feeling had been so strong that she had even begun a postcard to him, but perhaps it would be better not to send it quite yet.

Callie's eyes grew thoughtful as she stared up at the ceiling. It would be all too easy to fall back into the routine with Neil. He was very persistent, and there were times, as at Athens Airport, when she was half tempted, and if he had been a little less sure that she would come running back to him she might well have done just that. She was still fond of him, still admired him. She was grateful that her affair with Stefan hadn't ruined their friendship, but it was impossible not to feel an undercurrent of frustration that it had barely ruffled Neil's complacency. He had always been indulgent of her wistful dreams of romance and excitement, and clearly considered that Stefan was merely an example of Callie's disastrous lack of judgement when attempting independence.

It was hard to argue with that, Callie thought honestly, but she couldn't help feeling that if Neil had loved her he would have been hurt and angry about Stefan, and not, as Antonia had pointed out, downright condescending.

No, she would show Neil that she was determined to survive on her own. She wouldn't write to him yet. She would leave it a few days and then send a long, chatty, confident letter from one friend to another, about the island and the villa...and Jack Kingsley?

Jack.

Callie shifted slightly beneath the cool white sheet. She could visualise his face with a clarity that was almost a physical shock: the cool, curling mouth, the hard, exciting line of cheek and jaw, the tautly powerful body with its sheen of health, the devilry dancing in his blue, blue eyes. The mere memory was enough to make her nervous and edgy, and, in spite of her resolution of only minutes ago, she knew a fresh wave of longing for Neil, familiar, reassuring, reliable Neil. She knew instinctively that Neil would not like Jack.

Abruptly, Callie swung her legs to the bare wooden floor. She had made up her mind about Neil, and she didn't want to think too much about Jack.

Padding across to the window, she threw open the shutters and leant her elbows on the sill to breathe in the morning air, bright and sparkling like champagne. Outside, a grove of olive trees clung to the barren hillside, their trunks black and bent with age. The breeze lifted the narrow leaves and there was a ripple of silver as their undersides glinted in the sun, and between the branches Callie caught glimpses of sea, a deep, intense turquoise so vivid that it seemed almost unnatural to one used to the more subtle colours of England.

Sheer happiness came rushing back, and she pushed the thought of Neil and Jack aside as she pulled on a black swimming costume and a loose beige cotton shirt, and made her way down to the terrace.

The villa was still and empty; there was no sign of Jack. Callie told herself she was relieved and ran down the stone steps to the rickety jetty.

The sea beckoned invitingly. It was so clear that she could see every pebble, magnified by the light, which rocked gently with the sea. Dipping an experimental toe in the water, she grimaced. It was much colder than she had expected, but the deep crystal blue was irresistible and, steeling herself, she dived in, emerging at the last minute with a gasp and a joyous shake of sleek dark hair.

Above her, the sky was a vast blue bowl, and the light was diamond-bright so that the land stood out with unnatural clarity. From where she trod water, the villa seemed part of the hillside, half hidden by scrambling purple bougainvillaea and pink oleanders. There were lemon trees just beside the terrace, and the olives glinted silver in the breeze.

Striking out vigorously to warm herself up, Callie headed out into the bay. She had always been a strong swimmer and the sea held no fears for her. Indeed, she always felt at home in the water, almost another person, and she rolled and dived with unselfconscious grace, hoisting herself back on to the jetty at last to lie stretched in the sun, tingling with exhilaration.

It was hunger that made her pull on her shirt eventually and head up the steps in search of breakfast. Humming lightly to herself, she ran up the last of the steps to the terrace, only to stop dead at the sight of Jack Kingsley, lounging in a chair as he had done yesterday, his long legs propped up on the wooden table.

Callie felt very odd, as if all the breath had been driven from her body. She had remembered him so vividly, and yet still she was unprepared for the physical impact of seeing him again and her heart began to beat uncomfortably.

He was dressed as casually as before, in white polo shirt and khaki shorts, his legs brown and bare and his hands linked behind his head. Just sitting there looking at the view, he exuded such zest and vitality that Callie felt tiny goose-bumps rise on her skin, and she shivered, although she wasn't cold.

Jack looked up as she appeared, and raised an appreciative eyebrow.

'Well, well, the nymph emerges at last!'

His voice was warm, amused, and Callie suddenly became aware that her shirt had fallen back as she came up the steps, leaving her slender body in its skimpy covering exposed to Jack's interested blue gaze.

Hurriedly she pulled the shirt closed. 'I thought you'd gone out for the day,' she said stiffly, hating the way the glinting humour in his eyes unsettled her.

'I've been down to the shop to get you some breakfast,' said Jack, swinging his legs off the table to reveal a bowl of yoghurt, some honey and a dish of figs. 'You didn't have anything to eat last night, so I thought you'd be hungry.'

'Oh.' Callie pushed her hair behind her ears, uncertain of how to react to his unexpectedly thoughtful gesture. 'Well . . . thank you,' she said awkwardly. 'You shouldn't have bothered.'

'I feel it's the least Garth Havelock would expect of me,' he said with a grin, getting to his feet and pulling out a chair for her. 'Here, sit down and I'll get you a coffee.'

Callie sat down warily, overborne by Jack's sheer vigour. She wished he weren't quite so unpredictable. It was hard to know where you were with him.

When Jack reappeared bearing two mugs of coffee she took one with a shy smile of thanks, her heart jumping alarmingly as her fingers brushed against his.

'I've been watching you swimming,' said Jack, sitting down next to her. 'I've never seen anyone look so at home in the water.'

Callie reached blindly for a fig, still appalled at how disturbing such a brief, impersonal touch could be. 'The sea's wonderful here,' she said, hoping that her voice didn't sound as high and cracked to him as it did to her.

'You reminded me of a nymph the first time I saw you,' Jack mused, his eyes lingering on the dark sweep of downcast lashes against the smooth, pale cheek as she turned the fig in her hands, on the damp black hair smoothed behind her ear, unconsciously emphasising the fine bones of her face. 'A sea nymph, I thought; one of Poseidon's daughters.' His blue eyes glanced slyly at her. 'Well, I was almost right. Calypso might not have been related to Poseidon, but at least she was a nymph, wasn't she?'

The dark lashes flew open, and she jerked her head round, her eyes clear and grey and startled.

'Calypso?' She put the fig down carefully.

'Your namesake,' he explained kindly.

'Whatever makes you think that?'

Jack leant down and picked up a familiar blue and gold passport from the tiles beneath his chair. He waved it at her, grinning at her expression, his teeth very strong and white in his tanned face and his eyes alive with laughter.

'I had a look in your passport. You really shouldn't leave it lying around. Anyone might pick it up.'

'I didn't leave it "lying around", as you call it,' Callie said angrily. 'I left it in my bag. Do I take it you've been rifling through my things?'

'Just checking that you were who you said you were.' Jack was unabashed and Callie could only gape at the sheer nerve of the man.

'I hope you're satisfied now?' she said with cold sarcasm.

'Oh, yes, you are indeed Miss Calypso Anne Grey.' He flicked open the passport and studied the picture. 'Don't think much of the photo, though. The reality's much more enticing!'

Callie flushed as his warm eyes approved her, and she wrapped her shirt around her more securely.

'You've no business going through my personal belongings!'

'You admitted yourself that you didn't know Garth, and I can't help thinking that he would want me to check on perfect strangers turning up on his doorstep.' Jack assumed a virtuous expression. 'Anyway, I wanted to know what Callie stood for. Why don't you use Calypso? It suits you beautifully.'

'No, it doesn't.' What was it Stefan had said? 'Such a pretentious name for a little mouse like you!' 'I bet you wouldn't use a ridiculous name like that!'

'But I'm not dark and delicate with silvery eyes. I can see you as Calypso, keeping Odysseus enslaved with love for seven years.'

'He wanted to go back to his wife in the end, though,' Callie pointed out, and Jack sat up straighter.

'Calypso! Do I detect a touch of bitterness in your voice? Don't tell me you've been getting involved with married men?'

'No, I haven't, and don't call me Calypso!' She stirred honey crossly into the deliciously creamy yoghurt and tried not to think about Stefan. 'And please don't touch my belongings again!'

'I've found out most of what I wanted to know anyway,' said Jack, unperturbed.

'Don't hesitate to ask if you need any more personal information!'

Callie tried to sound sarcastic, but somehow it came out more petulant. Her hair, drying in the warm air, was falling forward over her cheek, and she pushed it behind her ears in a gesture of irritation. Really, Jack Kingsley was too much!

'All right,' Jack said equably. 'Who's Neil?'

CHAPTER THREE

CALLIE stared at Jack. 'What?'

'Neil,' he repeated. 'Don't say you've forgotten him already? You wrote him a postcard.'

Callie had been so taken up with memories of Stefan that she had been thrown by the abrupt mention of Neil, but now, too late, she remembered the card she had begun at Athens Airport. She had rested it on the stiff passport cover to write, and was forced to watch as Jack drew it out of the back, where she had slipped it when the flight was called.

With deliberate provocation he admired the picture on the front, then turned it over. '"Dear Neil,"' he read, '"you were right. I miss you already and wish we'd had a chance to say goodbye properly."' He waved the card at Callie. 'Touching stuff.'

Scarlet, Callie snatched the postcard out of his hand. 'I was always brought up to believe it was extremely rude to read other people's correspondence!'

'Postcards don't count. So who is Neil?'

'It's none of your business!'

'You said I could ask,' Jack pointed out reasonably. 'Is he your boyfriend?'

43

Callie had no intention of explaining the complexities of her relationship with Neil to Jack Kingsley. 'Yes,' she said firmly, hoping that it would shut him up, but she should have known better.

'Why isn't he with you?'

'He's working. He's trying to finish his thesis.'

'Oh, a student.' Jack waved a hand dismissively, and Callie's eyes darkened with irritation.

'Neil's brilliant,' she defended him, as she had so often to Antonia in the past.

Jack pursed his lips, and his blue eyes danced. 'He can't be all that clever if he lets a girl who looks like you go away by herself for a whole summer!'

'It's not a question of letting me do anything,' Callie said stiffly, on the defensive now. If only she hadn't said that Neil was still her boyfriend!

'If I had a girl who wanted to go away for three months I'd wonder how much she really wanted to be with me at all,' said Jack, watching Callie's face.

'Would you? But then, you're not Neil.'

'He must be a dull fellow not to wonder.'

'Neil is not dull!' Perversely, Jack's inquisition was forcing Callie to defend Neil on the very points she had her own doubts about. She eyed him resentfully. At this rate she would be talking herself into going back to Neil after all!

'So what is he like?'

'He's clever.' Callie struggled to conjure up Neil's handsome, rather earnest face, but it was a hard task with Jack's piratical features dancing in front of her eyes.

'And?'

'He's very calm, and—er—quite practical.' Too calm, too practical. Surely she could think of something else to say about him after five years? 'He's very nice,' she finished defensively, seeing Jack's expression.

'He sounds dull,' Jack said with satisfaction. 'Good-looking?'

That was easier. Curly hair, moustache, hazel eyes. 'Very.'

'And what's he studying that could possibly be more fascinating than a summer in Greece with you?'

'Politics,' Callie said, a shade sulkily. She could just imagine what Jack's reaction would be.

'*Politics*? He prefers *politics* to you?' Jack sounded incredulous.

'It's not like that,' she protested, even though she had frequently wondered the same thing. 'He can't just take off and leave his thesis after all the work he's done on it.'

'So he's quite happy for you to go on your own?'

'Yes.'

'He didn't try and make you stay? Wasn't he jealous in case you met someone else?'

'No.' Callie picked up her spoon and continued doggedly with her yoghurt. 'Neil would trust me in any situation.' There was a certain irony in that, considering how quickly she had succumbed to Stefan, but somehow it seemed important to impress upon Jack that she belonged with someone else, and that there would be no chance of her falling for the smile in his blue eyes.

'Ah, but would he trust me?' said Jack, unimpressed.

'He wouldn't need to.' Her eyes met his defiantly. 'He'd know that you're just not my type.'

Jack leant forward and there was a gleam in his dark blue eyes that Callie found hard to interpret. He didn't touch her, but under his gaze she felt herself grow suddenly hot, and without knowing why she put down her spoon uncertainly.

'We'll see,' he said.

Jack's lounging presence on the terrace made it impossible for Callie to concentrate on the Greek myths, and in the end she took her book and climbed up through the olive groves to where the pines cast a cool, fragrant shade as refuge from the midday heat.

Resting her arms on her knees, Callie gazed down through the branches at the vibrant blue of the bay spread below. All was quiet and still. Even the insects seemed oppressed by the heat, whirring in a desultory fashion somewhere above her head.

The page was open at the tale of Orpheus's descent into the underworld in search of Eurydice, but for once Callie's attention was not held by the story. Jack's infuriating blue gaze with its lurking amusement seemed to shimmer on the page.

How dared he go through her bag like that? And all those questions about Neil—as if it had anything to do with him! Callie's eyes glittered with renewed fury. Jack was so thick-skinned that it was impossible to snub him. Of course, it was typical of him to sneer at Neil. He wouldn't know where to begin to understand an intellectual like Neil, whose mind could encompass more than beer and women.

Here Callie's indignation wavered slightly as she remembered the keen intelligence in Jack's eyes. He might be lazy and frivolous, but he certainly wasn't stupid.

Unbidden, some words of Antonia's floated into her mind. 'You only think Neil's an intellectual because he's been telling you how clever he is for so long.' Callie shook away the memory. Neil *was* clever, anyone could see that.

Still, Jack's comments lingered aggravatingly. It was ironic that it took someone the complete opposite of Neil to make her appreciate him properly, Callie thought. He was so much nicer than Jack, so much less alarming. Why had she had such doubts about him?

She had known Neil since arriving at university to study fine art, timid and gauche, fresh from her country school. She had been terribly impressed by his air of assurance, flattered by a postgraduate taking an interest in a first-year; of course she had fallen in love with him.

They had stayed together throughout her three-year course, and when she had graduated it had somehow been taken for granted that they would continue to see each other at weekends. It was only when she got to London that Callie began to wonder whether she had missed out on some fun by tagging along after Neil, seeing Neil's friends, doing what Neil wanted to do.

Antonia had been more blunt. 'He's pompous and selfish. I don't think he even loves you. It just suits him to have you around as an audience.'

Callie had shaken her head, so used to defending Neil to Antonia that she did it as second nature by now, but the niggling doubt remained. Neil's qualities were obvious, particularly when he was compared to someone like Jack Kingsley, but she could see now that he didn't really love her. She hoped that her summer away would make him realise that too.

Mindlessly Callie turned a page. Jack would never let a girl of his go off for the summer, she found herself thinking. He might break her heart in the end, but he would never put up with a half-hearted relationship. He was an all-or-nothing man, of that she was sure.

What would Jack's girl be like? He had called *her* beautiful... Callie shook her head abruptly, not liking the direction her thoughts were taking, and decided to concentrate on the peaceful scene below her instead. She stared abstractedly down at the villa. A fishing boat was tied up next to Jack's, and two men stood on the jetty, conferring over a package.

Callie squinted through the branches of the pines, glad of a diversion. It was difficult to see from up here, but one of the men was obviously Jack. Funny that even at this distance he should already be so familiar. The other man, shorter and stockier, was gesturing to the far side of the bay.

Jack held the package now, and as she watched he glanced over his shoulder, as if checking that no one was watching, before he unwrapped it. It was a peculiarly secretive gesture, and for no reason Callie withdrew slightly into the shade.

Jack was nodding, clapping his companion on the shoulder, before turning and making his way up the steps, carrying the package very carefully. The other man jumped into his boat and cast off. The sound of the little engine carried through the clear air to Callie as she watched the boat disappear round the headland towards the port.

Puzzled, she sat back. What was that all about? Not for the first time Callie wondered exactly what Jack was doing on Pikos. She watched the villa a little longer to see if he would come out again, but the air shimmered undisturbed in the heat and eventually she decided to put Jack out of her mind. Getting to her feet, she shook the pine needles from her skirt. She had better things to do than think about Jack Kingsley.

It was late afternoon by the time she got back to the villa and the harsh light was fading from the sky. She had had a good afternoon. Inspired by her reading, she had made a good start with some sketches of the hillside, and detailed drawings with notes of the trees. One even had a satyr peering mischievously from behind the trunk. Callie had smiled as she had drawn. She was sure she would be able to use the scene somewhere.

Jack had left her a note on the terrace table, held down by an empty beer bottle.

Dear Calypso, Gone down to the taverna. See you there. Jack.

Insensibly annoyed, Callie screwed it up and dropped it in the bin. There was something about Jack that got under her skin. Even his handwriting, a bold black scrawl, antagonised her. It had much the same effect as Jack's physical presence, jumping off the paper at you, making you want to take a step backwards.

Her good humour evaporated and the relaxing afternoon was forgotten, as the note reminded her just how cross she had been with Jack when she had stalked out of the villa earlier that day. She would have done anything *not* to go down to the taverna, but a cursory inspection of the kitchen left her with little alternative. Jack's idea of housekeeping evidently went no further than keeping the fridge stocked with beer. Callie shut the door disapprovingly and went to change. There was no point in starving just to spite Jack.

It was nearly dark as she walked down the track into the port. To her surprise, the taverna was alight with music and laughter, and she stopped at the edge of the square. It was hard to believe this was the same quiet place where she had arrived only yesterday. Where had everyone come from?

Her eyes fell then on the yachts moored against the quay. There were about ten boats altogether, all with identical covers to their sails. The rigging chinked as the flotilla rocked in the slight swell.

Obviously a sailing holiday. Callie crossed the square to the taverna with some reluctance. She hated large, noisy groups and it sounded as if this one was already in boisterous mood.

She hesitated shyly in the doorway, but everyone was having far too good a time to notice her. Grouped around four or five tables, they all seemed to be tanned and blond, all young, all dressed in a variety of shorts and T-shirts.

In the middle of them all sat Jack Kingsley, telling outrageous jokes and flirting with a long-legged girl who kept running her hand through sun-streaked hair. Callie eyed her with deep resentment. She had always wanted to look like that, tall and blonde and confident. She was horribly conscious of her pale, London-winter skin and demure moss-green dress.

Catching sight of her, Jack called her name and waved his arm expansively to indicate that she should join them, but made no move to detach himself from his blonde. Callie smiled tightly and deliberately chose a table on her own in the corner.

She wasn't so desperate for company that she wanted to sit and watch him pawing another girl!

Determinedly aloof, Callie fiddled with her glass of retsina and watched Jack out of the corner of her eye. His eyes had narrowed slightly at her rejection of his friendly offer, but he didn't look exactly broken-hearted. Callie, uncomfortably aware of having behaved ungraciously, told herself that he was consoling himself more than adequately with the blonde girl, who was laughing far too loudly at his jokes. She was obviously mad about him, and Callie wondered, with an odd sinking of the heart, whether she was a permanent fixture in Jack's life. He hadn't mentioned a girlfriend, but there was something intimate in the way the blonde leant against him that suggested that they were more than just acquaintances.

What did it matter? Callie took a swig of her drink and told herself that she was miserable because she was missing Neil after all. The girl was pretty and clearly keen, and Jack *was* attractive, Callie admitted to herself grudgingly—if you liked that disreputable type. They were well suited.

Now he was singing! Good God, what next? Plate smashing? Callie sniffed disapprovingly as she ate her meal, aware that she was more than a little envious of the group having such fun, and taking refuge in snobbery. How Neil would shudder if he were here!

'Hi!'

Callie looked up, startled, to see one of the young men from the flotilla pull out one of the chairs from her table. He was dressed like all the others, in long, brightly patterned shorts, T-shirt and designer tan, but he had a square, open face and steady brown eyes. The sense of solid reliability reminded Callie oddly of Neil, and she warmed to him instinctively. Jack's absorption in his blonde girlfriend had left her feeling stupidly lonely and vulnerable, and the stranger's resemblance to Neil was reassuringly welcome.

'All alone?' he asked.

Callie had opened her mouth to reply when she noticed that for some extraordinary reason Jack was looking directly at her and frowning with unmistakable displeasure at the sight of the younger man hovering by her table.

Puzzled, Callie glanced up at her companion and then over to Jack again. The blonde didn't seem to have noticed that she had lost his attention, but Callie had no doubt that he didn't want her talking to the other man.

She smiled up invitingly, her welcome even warmer than she had intended. 'Yes, I am. Why don't you sit down?' Jack's glower of reaction was all she had hoped it would be.

'Thanks.' He smiled over the table at her, an open, friendly smile that went with his marked Australian accent. 'My name's Marcus Wilder.' Callie murmured her own name in reply and he went on, 'I'm in charge of that mob over there.' He jerked his head at the boisterous group around Jack. 'I wondered if you'd like to join us, since you're on your own?'

Callie was touched. It was nice of him to think of including her; it was more than Jack had done, after all. True, Jack had beckoned her over, but Marcus had gone to the trouble of coming over and talking to her.

'It's kind of you to think of it,' she said, 'but I'm really quite happy by myself. I'm leaving soon anyway.' She could feel Jack's eyes on her and struggled to keep her attention on Marcus. 'Did you all come in on the boats?'

'That's right. We run flotilla holidays for people who don't have time to sail their own boats out here. They fly out, cruise around the islands for a couple of weeks and then fly home again. We—the crew, that is—have to get all the boats from A to B without too many disasters and generally make sure that everyone has a good time.'

'They certainly seem to be having that,' Callie said with a glance at the laughing group. In spite of his informal attire, Marcus had a subtly professional air about him. What a contrast to Jack, who just lay around all day! 'How many crew are there apart from you?'

'Just Nikki. That's her over there.' Marcus turned in his chair to indicate the blonde girl draped over Jack, and Callie's eyes narrowed. 'She's really here to organise the social events and make sure everyone gets on together.'

'She seems to be very good at her job,' said Callie, watching Nikki toss back her hair and whisper something in Jack's ear, which made him laugh. She was certainly getting on with Jack.

Marcus didn't seem to notice the edge to Callie's voice. 'Yes, she's great. Everyone loves Nikki.'

Including Jack, presumably. 'Really?' Callie said coldly. Jack was still watching her with that strangely narrowed look and she wondered why. It could hardly be that he was jealous of Marcus, not when he had Nikki giving him her undivided attention! She changed the subject. 'I was quite surprised to see you here. I thought there weren't any tourists on Pikos.'

'There aren't really. There are no hotels, and just this one taverna, and the ferry only comes once a week, so you need to be pretty keen to get here. There aren't many beaches or any spectacular ruins to attract people anyway. It's different for us. We're self-sufficient on the boats, but we moor here quite regularly to give everyone a night ashore somewhere a bit different. We try and find good places for barbecues too. Some of the beaches on Pikos are fun because they're so hidden away and you can only get at them from a boat.' Marcus paused. 'What about you? Are you staying long?'

'About three months.'

'Really?' To her surprise he seemed to tense with interest. 'Where are you staying?'

'At a villa, round the other side of the headland.'

'On your own?'

'No, I'm sharing with someone called Jack Kingsley.' Callie nodded over to where Jack was sitting. 'You probably know him—your friend Nikki certainly seems to!'

'You're staying with Jack?' For a moment Callie thought Marcus sounded almost wary, but when she glanced at him he was looking genial and she thought she must have imagined it. 'Hey, that's great,' he said. 'We all know Jack, so we're bound to see you around. You can come exploring for barbecue beaches with us one day.'

Callie's eyes had slid over to Jack once more. He was laughing with Nikki. She thought she would rather die than spend a day in Nikki's company, but at that moment Jack looked across at her, and there was no mistaking the suspicion in his eyes. Disentangling himself from Nikki, he said something to her that made her watch him with a complacent smile as he began to thread his way between the tables to where Callie and Marcus sat.

Callie turned abruptly back to Marcus before Jack could reach them. 'I'd like that,' she said with a smile. 'Let's go soon.'

'We'll fix up a date after the next group change-over,' Marcus said, evidently pleased at her enthusiasm. He was sitting with his back to the group and was unaware of Jack's approach until the other man spoke from behind his shoulder.

'A date for what?' Jack sounded friendly enough, but his eyes were hard.

'Callie's going to come exploring with me.' Marcus got to his feet. His pleasant face showed no emotion, but Callie could sense the antagonism that lurked unmistakably beneath the civilities. He turned back to her with a warm smile, effectively excluding Jack. 'Nice to meet you, Callie. I'll see you soon, I hope, and we won't forget our date.'

'I'll look forward to it,' said Callie with a touch of defiance as she felt Jack's eyes on her.

'I could take you exploring, if you want to go so much,' Jack said as Marcus made his way back to the other tables.

'You don't need to entertain me.' Callie got to her feet and gathered up her bag. She glanced meaningfully at Nikki. 'You seem to have more than enough to do entertaining everybody else.'

'Just being friendly,' Jack said. The cold look had disappeared with Marcus, and the twinkle was back in his eyes. 'You don't object, do you?'

'Object? Why on earth should I object?'

Jack crossed his arms and regarded her with mock concern. 'I just wondered why you'd been looking so disapproving all evening.'

'I'm surprised you noticed how I looked,' Callie couldn't help retorting. 'From what I could see, your attention was fully occupied with your little blonde friend!'

'I'd have given you lots of attention too if you'd come over and sat with us,' Jack pointed out with a grin.

'I prefer to be on my own,' Callie said with an attempt at dignity. 'You're not responsible for me. I can manage quite well by myself.'

'I know you can. I just thought you'd enjoy the company. They're nice people.'

'I could see how much *you* liked them,' Callie said tartly. 'Or one of them, anyway.'

'Calypso! What can you mean?'

Jack's eyes were dancing and Callie was beginning to wish that she'd kept her mouth shut. 'I got the impression that you and Nikki would rather have been alone. You certainly behaved as if you were!'

'Ah, now I know why you were so disapproving!'

'I don't approve or disapprove,' said Callie loftily. 'I couldn't care less how you behave. We happen to be staying in the same place, but that's as far as our involvement goes.'

Seizing the opportunity to leave with the last word, Callie pushed past him, walked hurriedly over to the bar and paid her bill. She ignored Jack as she went out, although she couldn't help noticing that he had already returned to his seat and was nose to nose with Nikki again, so she made a point of giving Marcus a friendly wave.

It was very dark away from the taverna and she stood for a moment, listening to the creak of the boats while her eyes adjusted. A slight breeze rattled the rigging, and she wrapped her arms about her to keep warm.

She felt keyed-up and restless as she walked back up the hill. The moonlight was shimmering silver on the calm sea when she got back to the villa, and on an impulse she slipped into her swimming costume and ran down to the jetty.

The water closed over her like silk, cool and invigorating, and she turned in it, letting her restlessness dissolve in the still night. Phosphorescence glowed as she moved her limbs and she laughed in sheer delight, rolling and diving. Poseidon's daughter... perhaps Jack was right after all.

At length she struck back to the jetty. Absorbed in her own pleasure, lifting her head only to breathe, she didn't see Jack until she emerged, gasping and smiling, beneath his feet. He was sitting on the edge of the jetty, one leg bent, the other trailing in the water, grinning at her expression.

Callie's mouth dropped open at the shock of seeing him so unexpectedly, and she promptly swallowed a mouthful of sea water. Coughing and spluttering, she had no choice but to allow Jack to haul her unceremoniously on to the jetty.

'Not very elegant!' said Jack, laughing, patting her on the back, letting his hand linger on her cool skin until she jerked herself away. 'Just when I'd decided you really were a naiad after all!'

'What are you doing here?' Callie coughed, and scrabbled for her towel. Her back burned where he had touched her.

Jack's eyes rested on the pale, pearly sheen of her skin in the moonlight. 'Going fishing.'

'Really?' she said in an attempt at sarcasm, and glanced significantly around the empty jetty. 'With your bare hands?'

'Spiro's coming to pick me up in his boat,' Jack explained, unperturbed. 'I just came down to wait for him and see if you were still in a bad mood.'

'I am not in a bad mood!'

'Then why are you talking through clenched teeth?'

Callie didn't deign to reply. She concentrated on towelling herself vigorously to take her mind off the gleam of his smile in the moonlight. His shirt hung open and his bare chest was broad and strong. She wished she hadn't noticed.

'I'm surprised to see you back here so soon,' she said at last, when Jack seemed quite content just to watch her. 'You looked as if you were settling in for the night when I left the taverna.'

'For someone supposedly so uninterested in what I do, you're remarkably observant, Calypso!'

'Since you and Nikki or whatever her name is seemed determined to make sure everyone knew what a good time you were having, it was rather hard not to notice what you were doing,' Callie said waspishly, fastening the towel firmly around her.

'I suppose you'd rather we whispered together like you and Marcus Wilder? What did he want anyway?' He let his eyes travel lazily over her, lingering on her mouth and the warm line of her throat. 'Or can I guess?'

In spite of the cool night air, Callie felt a tide of heat wash over her, and she was passionately grateful for the dark, which hid the tell-tale stain of colour in her cheeks. 'I don't see that it's any of your business,' she said, 'but, if you must know, he was just asking if I wanted to join the group.'

'Why, had they come apart?'

'You're really very childish sometimes,' Callie said with as much dignity as she could muster between chattering teeth. 'I thought it was very kind of him to ask me.'

'I asked you, but all I got for my trouble was a cold shoulder. How come Marcus got all those warm smiles and lingering looks?'

Callie rubbed her arms against the chill. 'I don't know what you're talking about.'

'Don't you? I didn't even know that you could smile like that, Calypso. You certainly never smile at me in quite that way. What's so special about him?'

'Nothing,' said Callie, baffled and more than a little irritated by Jack's dog-in-the-manger attitude. 'He's just nice.'

'Oh, yes, he's very *nice*, is Marcus.'

'Why don't you like him?'

Jack shrugged. 'I just find all that niceness a bit cloying.'

'It didn't seem to bother you with Nikki,' Callie said tartly. 'She was being so nice to you that I'm surprised you even noticed what Marcus was doing!'

'You seem to have spent as much time watching Nikki as you did flirting with Marcus,' Jack commented, but when Callie refused to rise to the bait and only looked huffily away he went on, 'Her niceness is genuine. Marcus has to work a bit too hard at his.'

'Rubbish!'

'You obviously didn't notice. I suppose he reminded you of Neil?' Jack said nastily. 'All that niceness and reliability.'

'As a matter of fact, he did. And there's nothing wrong with being nice.'

'You would say that.' He eyed her moodily. 'You probably think everyone's nice.'

Nettled, Callie retorted before she could stop herself, 'I don't think *you're* nice!'

'Oh, I can be quite nice when I try,' Jack said, a strange note in his voice. Moonshadows turned his body into solid blocks of darkness and light, and it was impossible to read his expression. 'In fact, I can be really very nice.'

His voice was deep and warm, and Callie felt oddly breathless. She was suddenly very conscious of her own body, of the droplets of water on her shoulders, of the night air, cool against her skin, and the blood surging along her veins.

'I think I'd better go,' she said, horrified to hear her voice cracking. 'I'm getting cold.'

Jack was standing between her and the stone steps. The jetty was narrow and she would have to brush past him, but to her surprise he stood aside immediately. 'See how nice I can be!'

Callie didn't know whether to feel relieved or disappointed. Securing the towel around her, she gave an uncertain smile, and went to walk past him, only to find herself brought up short against an arm that felt as solid and unyielding as an iron bar.

CHAPTER FOUR

CALLIE'S mouth was dry, her heart thumping. 'Excuse me.'

'In a minute.' Jack drew her against him and he was no longer light and shadows. He was warm and breathing, hard and strong. Callie felt his heat burn her where his skin touched hers and a *frisson* of something—what? Excitement? Fear? Anticipation?—shuddered down her spine.

'Let me go,' she said bravely, but she was shocked at how husky her voice sounded. She rammed her hands against his chest, but somehow the movement only made her more aware of him. His skin was sleek but unyielding, like satin over steel, and her fingers spread helplessly as Jack pulled her closer.

His hand slid up from her waist almost impersonally to push up her chin so that she was forced to look at him.

'No,' he said, and there was a lurking smile about his mouth. 'I want to be nice first.'

To Callie it seemed an eternity that he looked down into her face but then, just when she thought he might let her go after all, he bent his head and kissed her.

His mouth was warm and persuasive. Callie closed her eyes against the fire deep within her that leapt in instinctive response, but it was useless. Even as her mind told her to pull away, a wave of excitement seemed to break over her, parting her lips beneath his, and slipping her arms around his as he tightened his hold on her and deepened his kiss. The towel slipped unnoticed to the ground, leaving only the thin, damp material of the swimming costume between them.

Spreading her fingers against his back, she gave herself up to the thrill of skin upon skin, and when his lips found the sensitive spot just below her ear she tipped her head back, felt her body quiver as his mouth teased her, drifting down her throat, exploring the smooth, luminous skin.

Jack's hands were at the straps of her costume when they stilled suddenly. Through a haze Callie heard the sound of a boat approaching the jetty. Jack put her slowly from him as he shouted something in Greek to the figure behind the wheel.

'Spiro's come to take me fishing,' he said in a perfectly normal voice.

Callie could only stand, shocked by the abrupt return to reality, her eyes huge and appalled with the dawning realisation of just how passionately she had responded to Jack's kiss.

'There, wasn't that nice?' Jack said, turning back to her and readjusting her straps with warm, unhurried fingers. He was grinning, apparently quite unaffected by the dizzy excitement of the kiss they had just shared. He bent and picked up the towel from where it had fallen, and wrapped it round her shoulders as if she were a child. 'I thought so, anyway.'

'You…you…' Callie froze, opening and closing her mouth furiously. How could he stand there smiling like that when her whole body still throbbed with the warmth of his touch? How could she have succumbed with such humiliating ease? No wonder he was smiling! She couldn't decide whether she hated him more, or herself.

In the end she took the line of least resistance, and with a glare at Jack's amused face she whirled round and fled up the stone steps to the safety of her room.

She was *not* going to succumb to mere physical attraction again! She had fallen once before, seduced by the thrill of a racing pulse, hoping for excitement and finding only pain, humiliation and guilt. She wasn't going to get hurt again.

Callie tossed restlessly beneath the sheet. It wasn't fair of Jack to amuse himself by kissing her like that. She didn't even like him. He *wasn't* nice. It was just that her heart leapt at his touch and her blood sang and her senses craved more. She could still taste him, still smell the warmth of his skin. Her fingertips tingled as if she could still touch the sleek strength of his chest.

She had come here to be on her own, she reminded herself in a kind of desperate defence. The last thing she wanted was to get involved with another man. She didn't want anything to do with

Jack Kingsley and the dangerous laughter in his eyes.

Callie fell asleep still trying to convince herself.

Determined not to give Jack the satisfaction of knowing how much his casual kiss had affected her, she decided to ignore the whole issue and carry on as if nothing had happened.

Even so, she had to steel her nerves when she went out on to the terrace the next morning to find Jack, lounging as usual among the geraniums. Callie could never understand how someone who appeared to do so little could emanate such an impression of energy. He was drinking a large mug of coffee, and, although his body seemed utterly relaxed, his eyes were on a small motorboat crossing the bay, and there was an unfamiliarly grim look about his mouth.

It vanished as he looked up and saw Callie watching him from the glass doors. 'At last! I thought all you artists were supposed to up and out with the dawn? Or didn't you sleep very well?'

Callie's chin went up. 'I slept perfectly well, thank you,' she lied. He needn't think she had lost any sleep over his kiss, even if she had lain awake into the small hours, remembering.

'There's some coffee here if you want some,' Jack said, indicating a jug on the table.

'Thank you.' Still formal, Callie helped herself to a mug, took a seat as far away from Jack as possible and stared determinedly out to sea. The morning sun glittered on the waves and the salt in the breeze mingled with the scent of the lemon tree that hung over the terrace.

Callie gulped at her coffee and wished she were not so overwhelmingly aware of Jack's relaxed strength on the other side of the table. She wished she couldn't remember the feel of his mouth in such detail. Glancing under her lashes at him, she saw that he was watching her with some amusement and scolded herself for having chosen a seat so revealingly far away from him.

'Did you have any luck last night?' she asked, in an effort to appear casual and unconcerned.

'Luck?'

'I thought you were going fishing?'

'Oh, yes.' Jack's eyes rested on her mouth. 'No, one way and another, my luck was quite out last night.'

Faint colour stole into Callie's cheeks and she looked quickly away.

'I thought I'd take the boat over to Ilonika to stock up on food,' Jack continued easily. 'Want to come?'

Callie hesitated. The last thing she wanted to do was spend the morning with Jack. On the other hand, the meal at the taverna had been more expensive than she had anticipated, and, even with free accommodation, she was going to have to be careful not to run through her painstakingly calculated spending money. It would certainly be cheaper to make some meals for herself, as well as picnic lunches and breakfast. She had glanced in the shop yesterday, but it didn't seem to stock anything beyond dry biscuits, bottled water and huge tubs of margerine. And if she wanted to go shopping on Ilonika she would have to go with Jack. There was no other way of getting there.

'Yes, I'd like to come,' she said at last, a little awkwardly. 'When did you want to leave?'

'Whenever you're ready. I'll wait for you down on the jetty—and bring a cardigan or something. It can be colder out at sea.'

Callie ran to her room for some money, remembering to grab a sweat-shirt just in time, and hurried down the steps. She was glad to see that Jack was already in the boat; standing with him on the jetty would have reminded her all too vividly of last night, just when she was doing her best to pretend that it had never happened.

It was a simple wooden fishing boat with an outboard motor. 'Is this Garth's boat?' Callie asked, for something to say.

'Yep.' Jack yanked the starting cord and the little engine roared impressively into life before settling down to a splutter. 'Isn't it grand enough for him?'

'It's not that,' Callie said, glancing about her. 'I just never imagined him to be the sort of man who'd go fishing.'

Jack grinned. 'Well, he's not very good at it, if that's any comfort! Did you think he spent his whole time here hunched over his typewriter?'

'I suppose so,' she said lamely.

'I'm afraid your image of Garth Havelock is wide of the mark, Calypso! He hardly ever writes here. This is where he comes when he doesn't want to be Garth Havelock, famous writer.'

Callie sat in the prow of the boat and turned her face up to the sun. The breeze blew her dark hair about and she pushed it away with her hand. 'Where does he live the rest of the time?' she asked. She didn't want to seem to be prying, but it was too good a chance to add to her meagre store of facts about her hero.

'Here and there.' Jack gave the engine a little more throttle. 'He's a restless sort of bloke. Never seems to settle down.'

'His family must find that difficult,' Callie commented, fishing, and, when Jack didn't answer, was forced to ask outright, 'Is he married?'

Jack settled himself more comfortably, stretching out his legs until they almost touched hers, and smiling at her, that lazy smile that accelerated her pulse-rate no matter how firmly she told her heart not to react. 'No,' he said. 'Perhaps if he met the right girl he might be prepared to settle down.'

'She might not want him to settle down. She might love him the way he was,' Callie suggested dreamily, thinking about Garth. She wasn't about to change her image of him, no matter what Jack said. He was the only hero she had. The bright light bouncing off the sea reflected in her eyes, so that they shone almost silver in the sunlight.

'You don't have a fancy to become Mrs Garth Havelock, do you? You sound just the girl he needs.' There was that odd note in Jack's voice again.

'Of course not,' Callie said with dignity, shaking off daydreams, determined not to give him any more fuel for his amusement. 'I'm in love with Neil.' It wasn't true, but at least it might shut Jack up.

Jack's face closed slightly, and he looked away from her to the blue, sparkling sea. 'Ah, yes, I was forgetting about Neil.'

Callie's hair was wild and tangled and her cheeks a-glow with wind and sun by the time they bumped gently against the quayside at Ilonika. Scrambling inelegantly out of the boat, she caught the rope Jack threw her and tied it rather inexpertly to one of the bollards.

Jack sighed as he leapt out next to her and insisted on showing her how to do it properly.

'I suppose Neil was always too busy agonising about the state of the world to show you how to tie a knot?'

Callie found it hard to even imagine Neil in a boat, let alone tying knots. She watched obediently as Jack demonstrated, but her attention kept wandering to his strong brown fingers, deftly twisting the rope. Last night those fingers had caressed her cheek, slipped beneath her hair to stroke the nape of her neck, burned over her bare back...

'Got that?'

With a start Callie realised that Jack was looking at her expectantly, and she nodded.

'You'd better be able to do it properly next time!'

Ilonika was hardly much bigger than Pikos, but they found a man selling fruit and vegetables from the back of a van who laughed and joked with Jack while Callie filled the inelegant plastic baskets he had produced from one of the kitchen cupboards.

Afterwards they wandered around a dark little store and bought a huge lump of feta cheese, jars of honey, great tubs of yoghurt, and tins of oily olives. Jack seemed to know everybody, Callie thought, inspecting a row of crackers, as he kissed yet another fat old lady and launched into the shouting match that he assured her was no more than passing the time of day.

'There's no rush,' he said, catching up with her and adding another tin of olives to her basket. 'Let's go and sit down.'

'We've got enough olives,' Callie protested, ignoring his suggestion.

'You can never have too many olives, Calypso.'

'Look, will you please not call me Calypso?' She banged her basket on the counter, glad of the excuse to be cross with him again.

'I can't help it,' Jack said impenitently. 'I keep thinking of you as a dark, elusive nymph, trapped on land and longing for the sea ... How's that for a bit of free analysis? Neil obviously represents the land, and the sea is all the fun and excitement you could have if you forgot all about him and let yourself go. Well, what do you think? No need to pay for a psychiatrist while Jack's around!'

'Is this all based on the fact that I like swimming?' Callie asked in a cold voice.

'It's based on how you kissed me last night,' Jack said with a sideways smile that curled his mouth and twisted her heart in reluctant response. Pushing her purse away, he paid the shopkeeper with his own money.

The warm colour rushed up Callie's throat. 'You took me unawares,' she accused him and pulled herself together with an effort. 'And I'm paying for these things!'

'You can pay next time,' said Jack, taking her arm and propelling her out into the street. 'What you need now is something to eat.'

He had an uncanny ability to stir her up and throw her into confusion just when she had decided to relax, Callie thought resignedly, allowing herself to be borne off to a small taverna on the waterfront where he was welcomed as usual like a long-lost son. And, having ruffled her up, he just carried on as if nothing had happened!

They sat at a table outside. Jack ordered tiny cups of Greek coffee and for Callie a *baklava*, oozing honey on to the plate. She felt much more in charity with him by the time she had finished.

'How do you come to speak such good Greek?' she asked, sucking her sticky fingers.

'My grandmother was from Pikos,' Jack said. 'My grandfather was an eccentric Englishman with a crackpot theory that Pikos was Odysseus's real home instead of Ithaca. The islands aren't unalike, so he wasn't as off beam as some of the theories, but he never found anything to prove it. He used to come here looking for ruins, but he only ever found my grandmother... He didn't do so badly: she was a wonderful woman.'

'Are there no ruins on the island at all?' Callie leant her elbows on table and cupped her hands around her coffee. 'Pikos must have been inhabited in ancient times, so it's not unreasonable to suppose that there would be some remains, surely?'

Jack shot her an odd glance. He seemed about to say something, then obviously changed his mind. 'There are some French archaeologists poking around on the other side of the island, but they haven't found anything very exciting.'

'What a shame.'

'Why do you say that?'

'If they found some really spectacular ruins it would really put Pikos on the map. It could be like Delos or Delphi, or Apollo's Gateway at Naxos...'

'Yes, and it could be ruined by tourism,' Jack said flatly. 'Pikos is happy as it is.'

'I thought tourism was supposed to benefit the local economy?'

'In my experience the only people who benefit are the big developers. They move in, put up a lot of concrete and push out the people who've lived in a place for years, or reduce them to a community of waiters and souvenir sellers.'

Callie had never heard Jack so vehement, and she glanced at him in surprise. 'Perhaps it's just as well there aren't any ruins on Pikos, then, in spite of disappointing your grandfather.'

There was the tiniest of pauses. 'Yes,' said Jack. 'Just as well.'

The short silence was broken by Jack saying, 'Hello, here's Spiro. Wonder what he's doing here?' A stocky man with a dark, lugubrious face was coming towards them and Callie thought she recognised him as the man she had seen hand Jack that mysterious package on the jetty yesterday.

She had forgotten all about the incident, and opened her mouth to ask Jack about it, but he was already rising to his feet and greeting Spiro, obviously urging him to join them.

Spiro sat and nodded gravely at Callie.

'*Kalimera,*' she tried. It was all the Greek she had learnt so far. He had rather a sinister expression, she decided. Definitely an odd friend for the gregarious Jack.

Spiro glanced at her and then said something to Jack that made him laugh. 'What's he saying?' she asked suspiciously.

'He said he could understand why my mind wasn't on the fishing last night,' Jack said with a grin, and she flushed.

'Oh.'

They plunged into rapid conversation, and although Callie couldn't understand a word it was soon clear that something was wrong.

Jack was frowning. She had never seen him look so serious before, she thought, stirring her coffee. It was almost like looking at a different man. He was leaning forward, putting questions to Spiro in a sharp voice. The laughing mouth was set in an unfamiliar line and his eyes were stern.

Callie remembered the way he had looked at her in the taverna last night, and a slight crease appeared between her brows. There was much more to Jack Kingsley than he liked you to think. The intent man sitting next to her, purpose written in every line, was not a man to cross, no matter how careless he appeared. She found herself thinking about his capable hands on the ropes. No, Jack would not be a man to let much stand in his way.

They were getting to their feet. 'Would you excuse us a minute?' Jack said to her grimly. 'I won't be long.'

'Jack, is something the matter?'

'It's nothing that concerns you,' he said brusquely, and Callie realised with a shiver that he was very angry. 'Just stay here.'

If he didn't want to tell her what was so important, that was his look out! Callie watched him walk off with Spiro, a little hurt. What was all the secrecy anyway? It wouldn't have killed him to let her know what was going on.

Rather huffily she got out her postcards. She wrote one to her parents, and one to Neil, carefully making no mention of Jack. She had just started one to Antonia when a shadow fell over the table.

It was Marcus. 'Hi! I thought it was you.'

Callie was delighted to see him. She had forgotten what a friendly, unassuming manner he had. 'I didn't expect to see you here,' she said when Marcus had sat down. 'What have you done with your boats?'

'They're moored a little further down. We're waiting for a new group to arrive tomorrow, so we're doing a bit of maintenance and restocking.'

'We're on a supply run, too.'

'We?' Marcus cocked an eyebrow at her.

'I came over with Jack . . . Jack Kingsley. You remember I told you I was sharing a villa with him?'

'Oh, yes. Jack.' For some reason, Marcus's smile made Callie feel uncomfortable. 'He was very proprietorial over you last night, wasn't he? How do you get on with him?'

Callie was still aggrieved at Jack's brusqueness. 'I don't see that much of him—and that suits me fine!'

'You obviously don't like him very much!'

Didn't she? Jack's smile seemed burnt on the insides of her eyelids. 'He's all right, I suppose.'

'He can be quite a charmer, can't he? He certainly knows how to handle women. Nikki's absolutely besotted with him.'

Callie's eyes narrowed fractionally. She didn't care for the idea of being lumped in a category of women Jack knew how to handle! 'He's not that nice.'

Even as the words came out, she was remembering him pulling her close on the jetty, his hands against her skin, his mouth against hers. 'I can be quite nice when I try... I can be really very nice.'

'You don't sound as if you like him very much, either,' she said on a half-gasp.

'I don't trust him,' Marcus said abruptly. 'Something about him doesn't ring true.' He gazed out at the fishing boats rocking gently in the harbour with a frown. 'He pretends to be just lazing around, but he's a bit too interested in everything, isn't he? And he doesn't *look* like a layabout. I can't quite put my finger on it. He's like a big cat, one minute purring in the sun, the next stalking its prey, all killer instinct. I think he's a dangerous man.'

Callie stared at him. His words had been an uncanny echo of her own thoughts about Jack.

'I'd give a good deal to know exactly what Jack Kingsley is doing here,' he went on. 'I don't suppose he's told you?'

'No-o,' Callie said slowly, remembering how vague Jack had been when she asked him what he did. She was still no clearer about his connection with Garth Havelock either. There was definitely something odd about that.

The more she thought, the more she remembered other things that had puzzled her about Jack. What about that peculiar incident down on the jetty, when he and Spiro had looked so surreptitious? And who was Spiro? He looked like a shady character, if ever she'd seen one! The first night she had been there, there had been a lot of activity in the middle of the night. They might have been going fishing, of course, but there seemed to be an awful lot of fishing trips without a sign of any fish being caught. What if they were up to something else entirely?

Callie bit her lip. 'You don't think he's involved in anything... well, illegal, do you?'

'I don't know,' said Marcus. 'There's just something about him that makes me uneasy.'

As he spoke he glanced up and nodded at a man passing the table. 'That's Philippe,' he said to Callie. 'He's one of the French archaeologists working on Pikos. Have you come across them yet?'

'No, but Jack was telling me about them,' she said absently, still turning over her doubts in her mind. For some reason she didn't want to tell Marcus about her suspicions, at least not yet.

Marcus shot her a sharp glance. 'Was he? When?'

'Just now.' Over Marcus's shoulder Callie could see Jack come out of a building and catch sight of her companion. He began walking towards them and even from a distance she could see he was displeased.

She looked nervously at Marcus, but he had glanced at his watch and was getting up anyway. 'I'd better be going. See you around, Callie—and let me know if you have any trouble with Jack Kingsley!'

Callie murmured goodbye, but her mind was on Jack. The mere sight of him made her suspicions seem ridiculous, and she was about to dismiss them when she saw him accosted across the road by none other than Nikki. Callie had forgotten that she would probably be around with Marcus.

She was standing now, a little too close to Jack, running her hand through her hair in that ridiculously affected gesture, laughing just a bit too loudly. Callie eyed her sourly. Jack didn't seem to be taking his bad temper out on Genuinely Nice Nikki. Instead, he put his arm round her and gave her a hug, grinning, and Nikki pressed against him, giving him the full benefit of her generous body.

Callie's lips tightened and she remembered Marcus's comment—'He certainly knows how to handle women.' Well, she wasn't about to be handled by Jack Kingsley! On an impulse, she pulled Antonia's card towards her and wrote quickly,

There is a very suspicious character called Jack Kingsley staying in the villa. I think you should check that Garth Havelock knows what he's up to—I have a funny feeling the answer may be 'no good'. Otherwise, everything is wonderful. Please thank Garth again for letting me stay. I don't care what you say, Antonia, he's still my hero!

CHAPTER FIVE

HASTILY sticking on a stamp, Callie slipped it beneath the other postcards just as Jack came up to the table.

'You seem very cosy with Marcus Wilder, Calypso.' His voice was sharp with suspicion, and if she hadn't just seen him all over Nikki she could have sworn he was jealous. 'Why are you so interested in him?'

'He was just saying hello,' said Callie defensively.

'Must have been a long hello. He was sitting here for long enough.'

'What if he was? There isn't a law against it!' Nettled, Callie began gathering the shopping bags together. Really, he had a nerve! One minute he was full of smiles and carrying on with Nikki in that stupid, infatuated way, and the next he dared to cross-examine *her* just because she had been having a perfectly innocuous conversation with someone else.

Jack seemed to lose interest in Marcus. 'Do you want me to post your cards for you? I'm going over to the post office.'

'No!' Callie put her hand protectively over them as he reached across the table. She didn't want him to see what she had written to Antonia. 'I mean . . . I'd rather post them myself.'

'What's the matter? Afraid I'll read your love-letter to Neil?'

'You didn't seem to have any qualms about reading my personal correspondence the other day!'

'Well, I promise I won't read anything this time. If a postcard is enough to tell him how much you love him, it won't be worth reading anyway!'

Callie gritted her teeth. 'I'd still prefer to post the cards myself, thank you.'

'Oh, well, suit yourself.'

Jack strolled off to the post office and Callie gathered up the cards angrily. If he had been less mocking of Neil, and less suspicious of Marcus, she might have been tempted to tear up the card to Antonia, but she was definitely going to post it now!

The journey home was a silent one. Jack seemed preoccupied and Callie, who had decided to be cold and aloof, was put out to discover that he didn't even notice her efforts to ignore him. She saw little of him for the rest of the day and he spent the evening with Spiro in the taverna, so she was left to enjoy a solitary meal on the terrace and persuade herself that she didn't mind in the least if he left her alone.

She was sitting eating yoghurt and honey the next morning when Jack appeared, yawning and stretching, dressed only in a pair of shorts. He had obviously had a heavy session with Spiro, Callie thought disapprovingly, but he was in high good humour and seemed to have forgotten his abstraction of the day before.

'Good morning, Calypso. Up with the lark, I see.'

Callie hadn't realised how much she had missed that tantalising smile. Her heart gave a queer lurch and she stirred her yoghurt ferociously.

'Good morning.'

Jack threw himself down in the chair beside her, leant across, dipped his finger into her yoghurt and sucked it appreciatively. 'Mmm, cool and refreshing. Rather like you, Calypso.'

'There's plenty more in the fridge,' said Callie, who didn't feel in the least bit cool. She felt hot and edgy, too aware of Jack's smile and Jack's strong brown chest and Jack's warm mouth sucking his finger.

'I'd rather share yours.' Jack helped himself to another dollop and sat back. 'What are you up to today?'

'Um . . .' Callie blinked and improvised rapidly. 'I thought I'd go for a walk.'

'Where are you going?'

'Oh, over there.' She gestured vaguely to the point at the far side of the bay, and tried to clear her mind of Jack.

'To the point?' Jack hadn't moved, but she had the impression that he had tensed, though she couldn't imagine what possible interest there could be in the rocky, inhospitable cliffs that dropped into the sea.

Callie sipped her coffee and looked at the point properly for the first time. Even in the bright morning light, the hillsides looked stark and mysterious, places where the gods might once have walked, and she felt a giddy rush of adrenalin as her fingers tingled with the need to capture the atmosphere in her drawings.

'It might be a good place to do some preliminary sketches.'

'It'll be a hard walk,' said Jack. 'There's not much of a path.'

'I think it'll be a worth a try.' Callie was enthused at the prospect. It was time she spent a little more time on the illustrations and a little less thinking about Jack. 'I might even be able to find a path down to that beach.'

'What beach?' Jack asked quickly.

'I think it's a beach. It's a bit hard to tell from here. Look, can you see that clump of broom between the two outcrops? If you go down and to the right, it looks as if the cliffs curve inwards, and I'm sure that glimpse of white must be sand. The rest of the beach must be hidden behind the cliff. Can you see?'

Jack following her pointing finger, and then his gaze came back to rest thoughtfully on her face. 'You've got good eyes,' he said slowly.

'I've got twenty-twenty vision,' Callie explained absently, thinking about what she would have to take with her. She'd need her sketchbook, of course, and it might be an idea to take some water and——

'Perhaps I'll come with you,' Jack said, linking his hands behind his head and stretching. 'I could do with a bit of healthy exercise.'

'With me?' she echoed nervously. She really needed to get away from Jack. It was easier to think she didn't like him when he wasn't there with his blue, smiling eyes.

'What's the matter? Don't you want me to come?'

What could she say? After all, he had offered to let her share the villa, and she didn't want him to think she was afraid to be alone with him. And it would be more fun if he came...

You don't want fun, a voice nagged inside her. You left Neil because you wanted fun, and all that brought you was disaster. You'd really rather be on your own. Wouldn't you?

'It's not that,' she tried. 'It's just that you'll probably be very bored. I'm just going to sit and draw.'

'I'm never bored,' said Jack, his long mouth quirking at one corner.

Callie could believe it. Those lazily amused eyes didn't miss anything, and she remembered Marcus comparing him to a big cat. Cats didn't get bored either. They just did exactly what they wanted.

'Anyway,' Jack went on, 'I think Garth would expect me to come along and keep an eye on you. We don't want anything to happen to you.'

'I'm hardly likely to get lost between here and the point,' Callie said.

'You can never tell. You've got a fey look about you, Calypso Grey. I wouldn't trust you not to get lured into the hills by the pipes of Pan, or transformed into a swan. Poseidon might catch you again, and take you back to the sea, and then where would I be?'

'You'd have the villa to yourself again.'

'It wouldn't be the same without you,' he said.

Draining her mug, Callie got abruptly to her feet. 'Are you ready to start now?'

The mocking glint was back in his eyes, but it was less unnerving than the look that had been there before. 'No, I'm not. I need some coffee first. What's the rush anyway? I suppose you were planning to set off without a thought to the essentials of life?'

'I just need my sketchbook...'

'And lunch.'

'I bought some crackers yesterday. We could take those.'

Jack shook his head sadly. 'If you think all I'm having for lunch is some dry biscuits, you're fair and far out, Calypso! Is that all Neil ever treated you to?'

'Neil,' said Callie with dignity, 'has far better things to think about than food!'

'The more I hear about this Neil, the more I dislike him,' Jack said after some consideration. 'But if his idea of a good time is to sit at home with dry biscuits and politics, it's his loss. You and I, on the other hand, are going to have a real picnic.' He hoisted himself to his feet. 'You just sit here, Calypso, and leave everything to me.'

It was an hour and half before they finally set off. Callie, left alone on the terrace, had half a mind to go without Jack and his precious picnic, but the morning sunshine and the fragrance of wild herbs drifting down from the hill did their work, and she was content to sit on and wait for Jack. It was quite nice to be looked after for a change. He was right, there was no rush. There would be other mornings as perfect as this.

A narrow path, not much more than a goat track, wound its way precariously around the steep hillside. Callie walked behind Jack, who had pulled on a white T-shirt, and tried to keep her eyes off his back. He was all long, clean lines, she thought, all easy, swinging stride. He seemed perfectly at one with his surroundings, even carrying that absurd bag, which looked as if it held enough picnic to feed an army.

Callie tried to imagine what Neil would look like here, with the turquoise sea on one side and the dusty hillside on the other.

She had a moment's panic when she couldn't conjure up his face, but then she pictured him as he had looked when they had said goodbye, a faintly pained expression on his face. No, Neil wouldn't like it here. He liked a roomful of books and people to argue with. He went to Edinburgh for the festival every year, and attended the occasional conference, but for the most part he was quite happy where he was. He wouldn't like the heat here, or the glare. He wouldn't like walking along a goat track, the spinifex catching at his legs, with only rocks and sea and sky to look at. He certainly wouldn't like Jack.

Callie's steps slowed until she stood still, staring out to sea. *She* loved it here. *She* liked Jack. Why had she wasted so much time pretending she didn't?

She knew why, of course. She had always been timid of life, and her experience with Stefan had left her scared. She had sheltered behind Neil, and if she hadn't found the courage to come away on her own she would probably have slunk back to his security in the end.

As it was, she was here and happy. Suddenly it seemed hard to believe that she had spent five years hanging on Neil's every word, impossible to imagine that she had ever been tempted to go back to him after Stefan. She had wasted so much time struggling to be the kind of girl Neil approved of when she should have known that he could never make her happy. Happiness was the sun beating down on her back and the scent of wild thyme heavy on the air and Jack, who didn't expect anything of her except that she should be herself.

'Calypso!' Jack had turned round further along the track and was looking at her strangely. 'Are you all right?'

Callie broke off a sprig of thyme and held it to her nose, savouring its pungent scent. She felt released, light-headed. The silky dark hair fell forward as she bent her head over the thyme, but when she looked up at Jack the grey eyes were silver-bright.

'I'm fine.'

They stopped early for lunch because Jack claimed he was hungry. 'I didn't have any breakfast, unlike some people,' he said virtuously. 'You were in too much of a hurry to rush me out of the house.'

'I don't remember much rush about it,' said Callie, thinking of the hour and half she had waited on the terrace, but she smiled as she tilted her face up to the sun.

'*You* weren't busy getting the picnic together,' Jack pointed out. 'I'm tired of carrying it now, and, anyway, you couldn't ask for a more perfect picnic spot than here, could you?'

Callie opened her eyes. A gnarled old olive tree shaded a flat rock high on the hillside overlooking the sea, which stretched flat and glittering to the horizon.

'No,' she said.

Jack had brought a tub of houmous from the taverna and some aubergine salad. There was crumbly feta cheese, still wrapped in its oily paper, wrinkled olives swimming in oil and herbs, a loaf of bread, rather hard and chewy, and sweet red tomatoes.

'Better than dry biscuits?'

'Much better!'

He opened a bottle of retsina while Callie sat cross-legged on the rock, hat tipped back, and bit into one of the tomatoes. The juice squirted out and she caught the dribble running down her chin with her finger. She felt almost euphoric. She had never known that a tomato could taste so good or that the air could smell so sweet.

The sun filtered through the olive branches, dappling Jack's face as he poured out the wine into plastic cups. The suspicions she had had about him yesterday seemed absurd today. Callie wished she hadn't sent that card to Antonia. She had been silly, making up mysteries about innocent fishing trips just because he had annoyed her about Neil.

Because he had kissed her, an inner voice amended, and because she had enjoyed his kiss more than she wanted to admit.

Marcus had said that he was a dangerous man, but as Jack held out the wine with a glinting smile Callie knew that the only danger was within herself, and she steeled her heart. She had been lured by the promise of excitement once before...

'You've been in another world all morning, Calypso,' Jack said, sitting down beside her. 'What are you thinking about so seriously?'

Callie picked up an olive leaf and twiddled it between her fingers. 'I was just thinking how beautiful it is here, and how glad I am I came.'

She thought that Jack might make some snide remark about leaving Neil behind, but he merely reached over and tucked a stray strand of hair behind her ear. 'I'm glad you're glad,' he said.

Callie quivered at the brush of his fingers against her cheek. Her eyes were huge and dark in the dappled shade as she turned her head to look at him. She wanted to say something, anything to break the silence, but could only stare into his eyes, conscious of her heart's slowing to a deep, insistent beat that thumped against her ribs.

The air between them seemed to tighten inexorably. Callie could almost feel herself being tugged towards him and then Jack looked away and broke the spell.

'Who had the foresight to name you after a nymph?' His voice was a little ragged. 'They could hardly have known you'd grow up to look the way you do.'

'My father.' Callie squashed a sense of bitter disappointment and told herself she was relieved. 'He teaches classics, but ancient Greece is his real love. He used to tell us the old myths as bedtime stories: I must have known them all before I could read.'

'Did the whole family get mythological names?'

'No, it was just me,' Callie said with remembered indignation. 'I think my mother thought my name was a bit silly, because Christopher and Colin got perfectly ordinary names. I always thought it was very unfair.'

Jack grinned. 'I'm disappointed. I thought you'd have an Apollo and an Adonis at least to share the embarrassment.'

Callie thought of her sturdy, practical brothers and burst into irrepressible giggles.

The taut atmosphere of a moment ago might never have been. They ate their picnic with unhurried enjoyment, talking easily, while the crickets whirred manically overhead and the sea glittered flat and calm under the midday sun.

'I should do some work,' Callie sighed reluctantly as she finished the last olive and licked the oil off her fingers.

'I suspect that there's a strong puritan streak beneath that fey exterior,' Jack said, stretching out lazily.

Callie pulled her sketchbook out of her bag and hunted for a pencil. 'I must make a start if I'm going to have the illustrations done by the time I go home.'

'*Go home.*' Her words seemed to ring in her ears. What would it be like going home and leaving the sun and the sea and the rocky hills behind? Leaving Jack? Already it seemed impossible that she should not stay forever.

But the whole summer lay ahead. Callie shook off the momentary chill and walked briskly up the hill to where she could look down on the olive tree and the cliffs beyond. She tried to recover the inspiration she had felt that morning, but her mind kept drifting back to Jack. He was sitting in the shade, lazily chucking olive stones over the cliff edge. How stupid she had been to even think he might be involved in anything underhand!

'Success?' Jack asked when she climbed back down to him.

Callie shook her head. 'Not really.' She didn't want to tell Jack she had been too busy thinking about him. 'A couple of useful details, that's all.'

'Can I see?'

She had found some myrtle on the hillside and had drawn it in loving detail, together with a straggly rosemary bush so clear that you could practically smell it. There was a drawing, too, of the olive tree, silhouetted against the sky. Beneath its branches she had sketched the outline of a man, the sparse lines somehow managing to suggest energy at rest.

Jack looked at them in silence, then closed the sketchbook. 'These are excellent,' he said at last. 'You didn't tell me you were that good.'

'They're just rough sketches.' Callie blushed as she put the sketchbook away, absurdly pleased by his praise.

'You shouldn't be humble about a talent like that, Calypso.'

Neil had always been faintly patronising about her art, Callie remembered, helping Jack to pack up the remains of the picnic. And she would never forget Stefan's comment: 'Don't tell me they're *still* teaching you to paint in this style? I thought it went out with painting by numbers!' No wonder she was humble. She hadn't had a lot of encouragement to build up her confidence, and she found herself wishing that she had met Jack a long time before.

'You're not going to leave that there, are you?' she asked, suddenly realising that Jack had left the picnic bag under the tree and was setting off without it.

'I thought we were going to find the beach? We don't want to be laden down with bags if we're going exploring! In any case, we'll have to come back this way. We can pick it up then. Nobody's going to take it.'

She must stop comparing Jack with Neil, who would have been horrified at such a casual attitude. Callie put her own bag back down in the shade and slithered down the path after Jack.

It was further to the beach than she had imagined. Walking with her eyes on the flowers by the path, she didn't notice that Jack had stopped until she literally bumped into him.

'Sorry,' she muttered as her body flamed with reaction, then stopped, following his gaze down to the tiny cove below them. 'Oh...!'

Almost encircled by the rocky cliffs, the beach would have been hard to spot from the sea. The water was deep and clear and so blue that Callie had to keep staring to convince herself that she was not imagining it. A crescent of white sand glittered in the sunlight, studded with once-jagged rocks, weathered now and rounded, like so many basking tourists.

'Shall we see if there's a way down?'

Jack picked a precarious way down the steep slope between the clumps of broom, and Callie followed, without pausing to wonder why she should trust him so absolutely. Her feet slipped once or twice on the loose shale, and Jack reached up with a steadying hand. At last he leapt down on to the beach from an overhanging rock and turned round to hold up his arms and lift her down.

Callie hesitated, looking down into his face as if seeing him for the first time. His eyes were blue and bold, his grin wide and white. His face was creased with laughter and there was a buoyancy, a zest about him that made the day alive and exciting. Succumbing to fate, Callie put her hands on his shoulders and let him swing her to the sand.

His hands were strong and hard through the thin cotton of her sleeveless T-shirt and she pulled herself quickly away and made a great show of taking off her shoes.

'Come on, let's have a swim,' said Jack.

'I haven't got a swimsuit,' Callie objected.

'Who needs a swimsuit?' he said, dragging his shirt over his head from the back. He was about to unfasten his shorts when he caught sight of Callie, who was looking flustered. 'Oh, very well, if it makes you feel any better, I'll keep my shorts on!'

'It's just . . .' How could she explain that she was having enough trouble controlling her imagination as it was? 'I don't mind what you do,' she said, a little crossly.

'Well, I mind what *you* do. You're too tied up with inhibitions, Calypso. How can you resist that water when you're hot and sticky just because you don't want to take your clothes off? You need to learn to live a little. Plunge in instead of tiptoeing around at the edge and wondering what Neil would think about it all!'

Jack sounded almost angry, and Callie opened her mouth to explain that Neil wasn't as important as she had pretended, but it was too late.

Before she realised quite was happening, Jack had scooped her up against his bare chest and was carrying her down to the sea.

'If you won't go in by yourself, I'll have to throw you in!'

'It's all right! I'll go in by myself!'

'Too late, Calypso. You hesitated too long.'

Callie tried to struggle, but his grip was unyielding and her wriggling only made her agonisingly aware of his bare skin against hers. He smelt of warmth and sunshine and dusty herbs.

Bracing herself to be dumped unceremoniously, she was surprised when Jack waded onwards into the deeper water. He stopped when Callie's feet were dangling in the water.

'I'm going to let you down gently,' he promised with a smile, releasing her legs so that she slid slowly down his body.

The water lapped up to her waist, chill against her warm skin, and she gasped, every nerve alive from the contact with his muscled strength.

'That wasn't too bad, was it?'

Callie shook her head, unable to speak. Jack's hands were on her arms, and when she didn't move they slid lingeringly to her shoulders. They looked very brown against her paler skin, which was only just beginning to acquire a honeyed warmth. The rippling sunlight reflected on the water and threw wavering patterns over their skin as it rocked gently with the waves. Callie's eyes were very clear as she stared up into Jack's face as if mesmerised. Her body ached with unspoken need as his hands drifted along her shoulders, his thumbs tracing the delicate outline of her clavicle.

He said nothing, but his eyes searched her face where her skin was glowing golden from the sun, and at last he slipped his fingers up her throat, burying them in her hair as he found her mouth with his own.

Callie sank against him without hesitation, her arms sliding round him to spread against his back. His kiss was fierce and she responded instinctively as he gathered her closer against his hard body, demanding as hungrily as he, giving as eagerly, with a glorious sense of release.

She was almost frightened by the searing pleasure of his mouth, the uncontrollable excitement of his hands moving possessively over her body, but she could not have broken away even if she had wanted to, and she arched closer instead, shaking back her hair and gasping as she felt him smile against her throat.

'I think it's time we plunged right in, don't you, Calypso?' Jack said, his lips wandering back to her mouth.

Callie shuddered with pleasure. 'I thought we were in,' she managed to say between kisses.

'We're only halfway in. I think we should go the whole way.'

And before Callie could protest she was hauled sideways, held tightly against him as they fell with an almighty splash into the sea and the cold water closed over their heads.

CHAPTER SIX

THEY surfaced at the same time, shaking the hair out of their eyes. Callie, whose mouth had opened in surprise at the last minute, had swallowed what felt like half the Ionian Sea, and was choking and spluttering, but it was impossible to resist Jack's face, alight with laughter. With his hair slicked back, he looked as dark and sleek as a seal.

'Beast!' she coughed, laughing, and smacked the surface of the water so that it sprayed over Jack, turning quickly before he had time to retaliate and heading out into the bay. The sea was like liquid crystal and the sun glanced off the rippling waves and into her eyes.

Jack caught her up easily, diving to pull her beneath the surface once more. Callie was ready for him this time, and their legs tangled languorously as they floated to the surface. Her arms were wrapped round his neck and they kissed, treading water, while his hands unfastened her shorts.

'Life's more fun in the deep end,' he said, hurling them on to the shore.

Callie was beyond thinking, beyond remembering Neil or Stefan or how she had vowed not to allow herself to fall for Jack. She was aware only of the solid smoothness of his skin and the spinning anticipation as he peeled off their clothes without haste and sent them flying out of reach to the beach until there was only water, cool and seductive, between them.

She felt liberated, as if the last of her doubts and inhibitions had been thrown to the shore with her clothes, and she entwined her body tantalisingly with his.

'Maybe you are a water nymph after all,' Jack said huskily.

Callie smiled, trailing her fingers over his nakedness, delighted and amazed at her ability to arouse him. 'I'm quite real. Don't I feel real?'

Jack pulled her closer. 'You *seem* real enough,' he said, running his hands over her in mock consideration. 'But I think I'm going to have to do a bit more research before I can prove it one way or another.'

They had drifted to the shallows, where the water was warmed by the sun, and he pulled her down with him on to the white sand. The waves broke gently over them unnoticed as they kissed, deep, hungry kisses that gained urgency as their hands explored each other in increasing need.

Rolling in the water, half laughing, half desperate, caught up in an unstoppable surge of passion, Callie gave herself up to the heart-stopping excitement of his touch, sobbing his name as his lips and hands moved over her in luxurious discovery, teasing and tempting, sucking and stroking, until her eyes were dark and dilated with desire and her body afire with a longing that the cool waves could do nothing to quench.

'You *are* real,' said Jack on a gasp, his mouth travelling upwards again, moving hungrily over her silken skin, savouring her sweetness. 'You really are.' Lifting his head at last, he held her face between his hands and looked down into her eyes with a wondering expression in his own. 'You really are,' he said again.

'I told you I was,' she said unevenly, shaken by the unguarded look in his eyes. No one had ever looked at her like that before and happiness surged through her before it was swamped in its turn by a deeper, more compelling force as their lips met in an unspoken acknowledgement of mutual need.

The sea lapped against the bodies entangled in the shallows, the sunlight danced around them. Callie shuddered with pleasure at the contrast between the cool, gentle water and the hot, hard insistence of Jack's body. His hands were more demanding now, and her body rose to meet him, open and warm to his touch.

The tenderness, the piercing sweetness faded before an ever-growing sense of urgency, and they turned and turned in the shallows with a kind of rough desperation. Callie's fingers dug into Jack's back as his mouth and hands plundered her body with a mastery that left her gasping with a delight so intense that it was almost painful. Her senses felt raw, as if Jack had unpeeled her to the very core, and this was the first time she had known what it was to really feel and really touch.

Jack murmured against her and she opened her eyes. The sky seemed to reel above them. If she looked down she could see Jack's dark head against her breast, moving lower, until his tongue's devastating exploration provoked a shooting flame of reaction, closing her eyes and arching her back in instinctive response.

'Jack!' she cried, pleading for release as she wrapped herself about him and let her body persuade him that the time was right.

Now he let himself be persuaded. Moving instinctively together, they gave themselves up to the final whirling excitement that pushed them higher and higher as Jack thrust deeper and deeper, carrying them onwards and upwards until Callie could go no further and surrendered with an ecstatic whoosh of feeling that spun out of control, leaving her dazed and breathless as she tumbled through glorious release and incredulous joy back down to the waiting white sand and the blue, blue sea.

Jack's face was buried in her neck as he lay against her, breathing heavily, and she stroked the powerful shoulders, her eyes wide and wondering.

'Jack?' she whispered as he stirred.

'Yes?' He lifted himself slightly to smooth the tangled dark hair away from her face.

'I didn't know...I'd no idea it could be like that.'

Jack smiled tenderly down at her. 'Sweet Calypso,' he said and kissed her mouth and then her throat. 'I always knew there was a wild, passionate creature longing to break free of that shy, uptight girl who got off the ferry. Poseidon's daughter... you're a child of the water, not of the earth.'

They shared languorous kisses, and then swam out to the blue depths without speaking, bound by a wordless happiness. The cool water slipped over their skin, clean and refreshing. Afterwards Callie spread their clothes out to dry on a rock and went to lie next to Jack on the soft white sand.

Stretching luxuriously, she thought that she had never known such happiness. Her body tingled, as if she had absorbed the sunlight dancing on the bright water. All of her senses seemed preternaturally heightened. It was as if she had never felt sand between her toes before, had never heard the gentle swoosh of waves breaking. She could still taste Jack's kisses and smell the salt and the sunshine on his skin.

He was totally relaxed beside her, his eyes closed, and a faint smile curling his mouth. Callie turned on her side to gaze at him, her dark head cushioned on her arm. It was good to be able to watch him without reservation, to let her eyes linger greedily on the body that had given her such pleasure.

He was all lean strength, and she could see the salt drying on his arms. This was not the first time Jack had lain happily naked in the sun, she thought. He was brown all over and the short dark hairs on his legs and forearms glinted golden in the sun.

Smiling, she lay back on the hot sand with a sigh of sheer bliss.

'You're not feeling guilty about Neil, are you?' asked Jack quietly without opening his eyes, mis-interpreting her sigh.

'No.' Callie closed her eyes too. 'I don't have any reason to feel guilty. I used to think I was in love with Neil, but I wasn't really. I realised that before I left.'

'Was he in love with you?'

Callie was silent, thinking back before she answered. 'I don't think so,' she said eventually. 'Not really. I think he was just used to having me around—but not too much, so that I didn't in-terfere with his work. It suited him quite well when I was living in London and I just saw him every other weekend.'

'He can't have loved you if he was happy to see you that rarely,' said Jack scornfully. 'How long did you put up with such a half-hearted relationship?'

'Over five years,' Callie admitted.

'Five years! Why so long?'

She let the sand whisper through her fingers. 'I'm not a very brave person, and I was terrified when I arrived at university, miles from home and not knowing a soul. I met Neil almost immediately. He was so at home there. He seemed to know every-thing, and it was easy for me to drift along in his wake. I suppose I hid behind him instead of carving out a life for myself. We fell into a routine and somehow things just plodded on until I went to London.'

Jack propped himself up on one elbow and outlined her mouth tenderly with one finger. 'What a waste of five years, Calypso! Didn't you ever think about what excitement you might be missing?'

'Yes.' Callie rolled over on to her front and began tracing mindless patterns in the sand. 'I discovered I wasn't very good at excitement. Antonia had a party one day and I met Stefan there.' She paused, remembering how she had first seen him. He had been talking to Antonia, blond hair flopping over his forehead. He had a thin, sensitive face, green eyes and an air of languid glamour that had made everyone else in the room look dull.

'He seemed to be everything I thought I was missing out on: clever, witty, dangerous. Antonia told me he was far too sophisticated for me, but I wouldn't believe her. I was determined to break free of Neil and prove that I could live as dangerously as everyone else.'

Jack was listening but he didn't say anything, so she went on after a moment. 'Antonia was right, of course. I was too naïve and inexperienced to deal with someone like Stefan. I was besotted with him. I used to sit by the phone, just in case he rang. I stopped painting because he told me I wasn't any good. I even stopped reading the books I liked because he used to sneer at my taste.'

'Who was this man?' Jack said grimly.

'He was something in publishing—probably not as important as he said he was.'

'I'll bet Stefan wasn't his real name, either!' Jack still sounded angry. 'Where did he come from?'

'I'm not sure. Somewhere in Surrey, I think.'

'There you are! He was probably called Steve and was just trying to give himself airs with a pretentious name.'

For the first time ever Callie could laugh about Stefan. 'He probably was! It certainly worked on me, anyway. He seemed so exotic compared to everyone else I knew. Things might have been different if I'd known he was called plain Steve!'

She dug a deeper pattern in the sand, her eyes dark with memory. 'I was very stupid about him, and I deserved to be made a fool of. Stefan found me amusing for a little while, and then decided he'd have a better time seeing how far he could humiliate me. It was awful at the time, but at least it forced me to make the break with Neil.'

'Serves him right,' said Jack unsympathetically. 'If he'd loved you properly he'd have made damn sure that no one else got a look in. How did he react?'

Callie sighed. 'He was terribly understanding. He said he knew that I'd wanted to prove my independence, but that really I needed the security that he offered, and that as far as he was concerned we could just carry on as if nothing had happened.

'I told him there was no question of that. Falling for Stefan had shown me that I couldn't have been in love with Neil, and if I went back to him I'd just be using him, but he refused to listen. He kept ringing and coming around and telling everyone that we were still a couple. He was like a steam-roller, and if I'd stayed any longer I'd probably have weakly given in to him. That's why it was such a wonderful opportunity to come here and get away. I was determined to cope by myself and have nothing more to do with men.' She turned her head to look at Jack, her eyes full of sunshine. 'I didn't bargain on you.'

Jack smiled, rolling her on to her back and brushing the sand tenderly off her stomach. 'I'm glad you told me about Stefan. At least I under-stand now why you tried to resist me for so long.'

'My track record with men isn't very good,' Callie explained, frightened that he would think her fickle.

Jack was unconcerned. 'Don't worry about it, Calypso,' he said as he bent his head to kiss her. 'You can't go wrong with me. You know what they say...third time lucky!'

Callie slipped her arms around his neck and pulled him closer so that she could kiss him back, a long, lingering kiss that told him better than words could how much he meant to her. She had carried Stefan around as an unpleasant memory for too long. Telling Jack had exorcised the hurt and hu-miliation. She wouldn't even remember him as ex-citing now, not since this afternoon with Jack, when she had learnt what excitement could be.

'You're all sandy,' said Jack, lifting his head at last for breath and running his hand proprietorially over her slender thigh.

'So are you,' she said indistinctly as his lips encountered the soft curve of her breast.

'I think it's time we went swimming again,' he murmured when the kisses and caresses that had begun so tenderly began to burn out of control.

The sea washed them smooth, cooling their ardour for only an instant before they sank back into the shallows, rediscovering the joys of touch and taste and feeling as if it were the first time again.

Later, much later, they sat curling their toes in the sand and let the warm air dry the droplets of water still trickling over their skin.

'We'd better go soon,' Jack said reluctantly, squinting up to note the position of the sun.

'Must we?' said Callie, but she allowed him to pull her to her feet.

Her clothes had dried stiff with salt, but she hardly noticed as she put them on. She was too content, too replete with sunshine and loving to care about a little discomfort.

She tucked her sleeveless T-shirt into her shorts and combed out her sleek dark hair as best she could. Her head was bent as she concentrated on tugging her fingers through the tangles, but when she had finished she looked up and pushed it behind her ears like a little girl. Her skin glowed and the huge grey eyes were startlingly light against her deepening tan. They were alight with love as she smiled at him, and Jack, who had been staring at her with a peculiar expression on his face, appeared suddenly to make up his mind.

'I want to show you something,' he said abruptly.

Callie looked about her in surprise. There were the rocks, there was the glittering sand and the still sea. There was Jack, watching her with that strange look in his eyes. He had dressed too, but there was nothing of him she hadn't already seen! Nothing had changed, except perhaps herself. She would never be the same after this afternoon.

'Show me what?'

'Come with me.' Jack held out his hand and she took it, feeling her heart stir anew as his fingers closed protectively around hers.

He led her to the far corner of the beach, where the cliffs were in shadow. 'There isn't anything here,' said Callie, puzzled.

'Isn't there?'

A flat piece of rock jutted out at an angle to the cliff, and to Callie's amazement Jack took her over and showed her a narrow crevice hidden behind it.

'You'd never find it unless you were looking for it, would you?' he said, dropping her hand to squeeze behind the rock and into the crevice.

'Jack! What are you doing?'

Jack turned round at the entrance to the crevice, where there was more room. 'I'm going to show you something I swore I'd never show anyone,' he said, suddenly serious. 'But before I do I want you to swear you'll never tell anyone else about it.'

Callie stared at him, wide-eyed. 'What is it?'

'You'll see in just a minute. Do you promise?'

Callie thought of all he had given her that day. A promise wasn't much to ask in return. 'I promise.'

'Come on, then.' The reckless glint was back in his blue eyes, beckoning her on.

Still she hesitated, peering into the dark depths of the crevice. 'Is it safe?'

'Come *on*, Calypso! Think of it as an adventure!'

Squeezing cautiously behind the rock, Callie followed him into the darkness. The crevice widened slightly after a couple of feet, but it was still too narrow to walk properly, and they had to edge sideways, Callie clinging nervously to Jack's hand.

'How did you find this place?' she asked, not realising that she was whispering.

'Haven't I told you we used to come and spend summers on the island as kids? I found it then, quite by accident.'

It seemed strange to keep this horrible passageway a secret for so long, Callie thought, fighting down a sense of claustrophobia. 'Is it much further?'

'We're almost there,' said Jack, and the next moment they burst out into the light. At first Callie could only stand and blink at the brightness, dazzled by the light after the pressing darkness of the passageway.

As her eyes adjusted she saw that they were standing in what had once been a vast grotto. Some time in aeons past, part of the roof had collapsed, and the sun poured down as if through a funnel, all the more intense for the contrast with the claustrophobic darkness from which she had emerged. Callie felt as if she was being drenched in golden sunshine.

Overhead, the rocks curved into a jagged vault, dipping down to the low tunnel that led out to the open sea. The water slipped beneath it, and the waves sucked and sighed quietly against a tiny strip of sand, as cool and clear as glass. Away from the funnel of light, the rugged rock walls stretched back into dark hiding-places, giving the place an air of quiet secrecy.

Callie stood, enveloped in silence, hardly daring to breathe in case she spoilt the aura of timeless magic that hung in the still air, but her hand tightened around Jack's.

'It's beautiful!'

He nodded, smiling, obviously pleased at her reaction.

'It's as if we're the only people who've ever been here. Do you think we are?'

'No,' said Jack. 'Someone was here long before us.'

There was a rocky ledge around the grotto, and he led her round to where it formed a platform above the sand and out of reach of the sea.

Following him obediently, Callie stopped dead, stunned by what she saw.

It wasn't a platform at all. Carefully built into the hollow of the rock was a mosaic in almost perfect condition. The colours were faded with time but the simple design was as vibrant as it must have been the day it was laid.

In the middle sat Poseidon with his trident, encircled by leaping dolphins. Tiny fish swam in an intricate pattern around the edge of the mosaic, and the god's attendant nymphs danced in each corner.

Jack looked down at their frozen dance thoughtfully. 'This one reminds me of you,' he said, pointing to a dark-haired nymph looking shyly over her shoulder. 'I thought so the first time I saw you.'

Callie looked from the mosaic to Jack and then back to the mosaic again, hardly able to grasp what she was seeing.

'It's . . . it's exquisite!'

'I know.' Jack was still looking down at the nymph.

'I don't understand . . . what's it *doing* here?'

'I think it was some kind of temple to Poseidon,' Jack said. 'But we can only guess, of course. It might have been built when the old religion was banned, but perhaps they just chose this place because it's such an obvious setting to make an offering to the sea. I'm sure it was used for some kind of ritual, because there are some of the jugs and bowls they used to use for pouring libations over there.'

Peering into the shadows, Callie could see the outlines of pottery and some larger pieces lying in the fine, dry sand.

'Is that a statue?' Ridiculously she found herself whispering again.

'A very small one. There are a few of them. Look at this.' Jack reached over and picked up a small figure, holding it reverently, and a memory flashed into Callie's mind of seeing him holding something else... She frowned, but the memory had vanished, and she put it out of her mind. It didn't matter, anyway.

She bent over the little statue, marvelling at the exquisite detail of the carving. It was a boy, standing poised as if about to take flight. His stone eyes stared at some unseen horizon and his mouth was curved in a tiny, enigmatic smile as if he saw something amusing there but didn't intend to share the joke. The artist in Callie ached at the sheer beauty of him.

'He must be priceless!'

Jack laid the figure carefully back in its resting place. 'It's going to stay priceless,' he said.

'But Jack, you can't really mean to keep this to yourself!' Callie exclaimed.

'Why not? I have for nearly thirty years.'

'Think how valuable it is!'

'It's not valuable until people know about it,' Jack said bitterly. 'Then it becomes a marketable commodity, going to the highest bidder.'

Callie bit her lip. 'I don't agree. This is more than a commodity. It's great art, and great art belongs to everyone. It's wrong to keep it to yourself.'

'I'm not keeping it to myself.' There was an edge of irritation to Jack's voice. 'I'm leaving it where it belongs. If we tell people about this the first thing that happens is that it'll all be taken away. It'll be photographed and split up and sent to city museums where the public will queue up to gawk at it behind glass without ever thinking that it should be here, where it was meant to be.' He gestured towards the mosaic. 'Look at it, Callie! Think of all the trouble they went to to build it here for the gods. Who are we to say it doesn't belong to the gods any longer?'

Taken aback by his unaccustomed vehemence, Callie stared doubtfully down at the mosaic. It was a great piece of art. She was an artist too, in her own unassuming way, but she knew she would not have been if she had not been inspired by the hours she had spent wandering around art galleries and museums, enthralled by such works of genius as this. Would this mosaic inspire anyone, lying alone for another three thousand years?

And yet she understood what Jack meant. It would be sacrilege to break up the timeless peace of this ancient place.

'Does anyone else know about it?'

'Spiro knows. My grandmother certainly knew. I told her what I had found, and she told me to keep it as my secret. I suspect that most of the islanders know. There must have been a story handed down through the generations, and those who have seen this place for themselves choose to leave it undisturbed. I think they're right.'

Callie hesitated still, and Jack said with some urgency, 'You mustn't tell anyone about this, Calypso. You promised you wouldn't tell.'

She nodded slowly. 'Yes, I promised. I won't tell.'

'Good girl.' He smiled at her, and for Callie that was enough. 'We should go. We don't want to be walking back along the cliff-tops in the dark.'

With a last look round the grotto Callie followed Jack back through the narrow passageway. Reaching the beach again was like stepping back into the real world.

Jack ran over to retrieve her straw hat from the shore and Callie followed more slowly, still thinking about the mosaic.

'Jack?'

He came towards her, spinning the hat on a finger. 'Yes?'

'Thank you.'

He handed her the hat with a flourish. 'It's a pleasure.'

'No, I don't mean for the hat.' She studied the hat, twisting it in her hands, then looked up at Jack, her grey eyes clear and direct. 'I meant thank you for showing me the grotto.'

Jack picked up a stray strand of hair and smoothed it tenderly away from her face. 'You're the only person I've ever wanted to share it with.'

'Really?' she said, a little shyly.

'Really,' he confirmed gravely, his fingers lingering on her cheek. 'I wasn't going to show you, you know. I thought it would be easier to keep it a secret if I never told anyone, but this afternoon...' The look in his eyes told he was remembering the golden hours of joy they had shared. 'This afternoon was special, wasn't it?'

Callie nodded. 'Yes, it was. Very special.'

'Perhaps showing you the grotto was my way of thanking *you*.'

They smiled at each other in silence for a long moment, and then Jack took the hat from where it hung forgotten in her hands and placed it squarely on her head.

'Come on,' he said. 'Let's go.'

CHAPTER SEVEN

THE harsh glare was fading from the sky as they climbed up to the cliff path and made their way back to the villa.

They talked little, but whenever Jack touched her arm to help her over an awkward bit, whenever he turned and smiled, Callie felt the glow simmering within her leap into a flame of remembrance: his brown hands on her body, his lips burning patterns of desire on her skin, the look in his eyes as he kissed her.

She felt dazed and dreamy as the memories circled through her mind. Sometimes she thought about the strange, fantastic place Jack had shown her, hidden deep within the cliff, but it meant less to her than the long hours they had spent lying in the shallows with the sun and the sea the only witnesses to their loving.

The picnic in the shade of the olive tree seemed a lifetime ago to Callie, but the bags were still where they had left them, just as Jack had said they would be. They sat on the rock and looked out to sea while they rested, their legs stretched out in front of them.

'Look!' Callie shaded her eyes and pointed to the horizon. 'That looks like a group of yachts. Do you think it's Marcus's flotilla?'

'Could be.' Jack's eyes were narrowed, but it might have been because they were looking into the sun. 'They look as if they're heading to Pikos. They were due to pick up a new group in Ilonika today and Nikki said they might make this their first stop.'

Callie had forgotten about Nikki, Nikki who was tall and blonde and glamorous, who sat too close to Jack and laughed at all his jokes. Her heart contracted with jealousy.

'Does she stay with the flotilla all year?' she asked in what she hoped was a casual voice, but really wondering how long Nikki had known Jack.

'Just the summer season,' said Jack absently, still watching the boats. 'She spends the winter in a skiing resort, working as a chalet girl.'

'Not a great career girl, then?' Callie said, resenting the fact that Jack clearly knew everything about Nikki and unable to prevent the waspish note to her voice.

'Nikki has a career in life,' Jack said with affectionate amusement. Callie wasn't sure whether it was at her expense or Nikki's, and decided not to pursue the subject, unwilling to hear how much Jack liked the other girl. She despised herself for her stupid jealousy. Surely she had no need to worry about Nikki after this afternoon?

It was almost dark by the time they got back to the villa and Callie was glad by then to have a shower to wash the salt and the sand from her hair. She stood under the spray, luxuriating in an unfamiliar sensuousness. Her body felt sleek, her skin had a new sheen and her newly washed hair swung clean and shining about her face. She could smell the almonds in the shampoo as she slipped a dress over her head and looked at herself in the mirror.

The dusky pink dress flattered the new warmth in her skin, and the soft cotton brushed suggestively against her body as she moved. Her eyes glowed, luminous in her tanned face, and she wondered if Neil would even recognise her if he saw her now.

Jack was whistling tunelessly in the shower as she went downstairs, and she smiled as she tied an apron around her. The kitchen looked more lived-in since their shopping trip to Ilonika—was it only yesterday?—and the fridge was bulging, but in the end she decided on a simple meal of grilled chicken and salad.

They ate on the terrace, with the moonlight shimmering silver on the sea below. Callie found an old candle in the depths of a drawer, and its flickering flame threw dancing shadows on their faces as the scent of the lemon trees drifted through the darkness.

Callie was thinking about how much had changed between them since they had sat there that morning. 'I wonder what would have happened if I'd never suggested going for that walk,' she sighed dreamily.

'We would have made love somewhere else,' Jack said with a grin. 'I was determined to tag along wherever you were going!'

'Is that why you pretended not to recognise the beach when I pointed it out?'

'I always thought you couldn't see it from here unless you were looking for it, and even then it's quite hard to spot. I reckoned without your twenty-twenty vision!'

Callie helped herself to a lettuce leaf and ate it while she looked thoughtfully at Jack. 'Even if I'd found the beach by myself, I'd never have spotted that crevice. I would certainly never have been brave enough to see if it led to anything.'

'Perhaps not. But you might have taken other people there, and they might not be as cautious as you.' Jack swirled the wine in his glass. 'I know you think I'm being stupidly secretive, but it's so important that nobody outside Pikos finds out about it. I shouldn't really have shown you, but I thought you would understand.'

'I do understand, Jack. At least, I think I do. I was remembering what you said on Ilonika about not wanting a rush of tourists spoiling Pikos. I suppose you were thinking of the grotto then?'

Jack nodded. 'There's still a danger that those French archaeologists discover something, but at least they're working on the other side of the island.'

'Did your grandfather know about the grotto, Jack?' Callie leant her elbows on the table and propped her chin in her hands. 'Think what fuel it would have been for his theory!'

'He would have been beside himself with excitement!' Jack said reminiscently. 'I suspect that's why my grandmother never told him. He'd never have been able to keep it to himself.'

'Poor old Grandfather. Weren't you ever tempted to tell him?'

'He died before I found the grotto. Otherwise, yes, I might have told him, just to watch his face. I'll never forget your expression this afternoon—and I don't mean just when you saw the mosaic!' He pushed back his chair and held out his arms. 'Come here.'

Callie went.

'You were so beautiful, Calypso,' he said, pulling her down on to his lap and kissing the pulse below her ear. 'You're beautiful now.'

Callie melted against him. His fingers were tangled in her hair, and he trailed slow kisses along her jaw until he reached her mouth. She opened herself to him, returning kiss for kiss, slipping her arms around his neck to pull him closer.

The fragrant night enfolded them as they clung together. There was no urgency now, no haste. They explored each other's mouths with teasing tongues, and found new places to touch that produced a gasp of arousal and kindled the slow, steady burn.

'Jack?'

'Mmm?' Jack was kissing her throat, his hand sliding beneath her dress to stroke the smooth, warm length of her thigh.

'I did something awful.'

'What?' he mumbled against her ear.

'When we were on Ilonika...I was cross with you.' Callie was having trouble talking with Jack's lips and hands playing havoc with her senses.

'You were cross with me all the time,' Jack pointed out, and she could feel him smile against her hair.

'The thing is...I sent a card to Antonia,' she confessed at last. 'I told her you were a suspicious character and that she ought to tell Garth Havelock what you were up to.'

'So?' said Jack, not sounding very perturbed.

'Don't you see?' Callie said worriedly. 'He might come back and ask you to leave, and it would be all my fault. Do you think I should write and tell her it was all a mistake?'

'No, I shouldn't do that. Garth might hotfoot it back and then you'd get a chance to meet your hero at last!'

'I don't want to meet him. I want it to stay just the two of us.'

'So you want to keep Garth out of his own villa? Some fan you are, Calypso Grey!'

'You're laughing at me!' accused Callie, catching the amused note in his voice. 'Won't you mind if he throws you out?'

'Not if you'd come with me.' His arms tightened about her. 'Would you?'

'Yes.'

'Just like that? What happened to the Calypso who hesitated at the very thought of adventure?'

Callie laid her palm against his cheek. 'You happened,' she said simply.

'Calypso.' Jack took her hand and kissed the palm tenderly. 'There's something I have to tell you . . .'

But she never learnt what it was. As Jack paused, searching for the right words, the peace of the night was broken by the sound of a boat approaching at speed.

A moment later the engine cut out, someone jumped on to the wooden jetty and footsteps ran along and up the stone steps.

'Damn!' Jack tipped Callie gently off his knee and stood up as Spiro burst on to the terrace.

It was clear even to Callie that something was badly wrong. Spiro was shouting and gesticulating, and so beside himself with anger that he could barely manage to answer Jack's sharp questions.

Jack was looking grim. Spiro was obviously urging him to some action, for he hesitated, and then turned back to Callie.

'I have to go. I'm sorry, Calypso, but this is important.'

'Is it to do with the grotto?'

Jack stopped dead. 'Why do you say that?'

'Because it's the only thing you think is important,' Callie said, standing tense and frustrated by the table. If only she knew what was going on!

Jack came back and took her face in his hands. 'It's not the only important thing, Calypso,' he said with a brief, fierce kiss on her lips. 'I can't tell you any more now. I'm sorry.' He smiled slightly as his fingers caressed her cheek.

He was gone before she could ask him any more.

Left alone, she slumped miserably in a chair and contemplated the remains of the meal. Why wouldn't he tell her? Didn't he trust her?

Sighing, Callie began to clear away the plates. She wished she knew what the sinister-looking Spiro was doing mixed up with Jack. She was sure it was connected to the grotto that Jack was so obsessively secretive about. Jack had said that Spiro knew about it, but, if he could trust a shady character like Spiro, surely he could trust her?

She was about to put away the tall salt and pepper mills when she stopped. They were about the same size as the statue of the boy Jack had shown her that afternoon, and all of a sudden she remembered when she had seen him handling something in the same reverent manner.

It had been on her first day here, when she had sat up on the hill and seen the furtive exchange between Jack and Spiro on the jetty. What had been in that package? Whatever it was, it must still be here in the villa, because Jack had hardly had a chance to do anything with it since then.

Callie put the mills slowly back on to the table. She was sure that the package would give her a clue to all the mystery. *Could* Jack have one of the statues from the grotto hidden here? But why, when he had been so vehement about leaving the grotto untouched?

Unwanted, an unpleasant idea was forming in her mind. She tried to dismiss it, but it nagged at her irritatingly. Was it possible that Jack and Spiro were planning to strip the grotto of its hidden treasures and sell them on the black market? It would explain why they were so concerned to keep it a secret. Jack had said himself that he wouldn't have taken her to the beach if she hadn't spotted it for herself.

And what did she really know of Jack? Only his lean brown body and the warmth in his eyes and the recklessness in his smile.

No, she was being silly! Callie picked up the mills again. Jack wouldn't be involved in anything like that.

What if he was? a little voice whispered. *Shouldn't you know?* It wouldn't change anything. She wouldn't tell Garth Havelock. She would still give up everything to go with him if he asked her. She just wanted to know.

Should she look for the mystery package while Jack was out? It was probably just a bottle of whisky and she would feel ridiculous. But at least she would know.

Callie dithered by the table. She put down the mills, deciding to look, then picked them up, deciding to put the whole idea out of her mind.

'Oh, this is stupid!' she said at last, exasperated by herself. It was better to know than to carry on speculating like this.

She felt uncomfortable looking through the drawers and cupboards, but, having made her decision, she was determined to find out what the package was. She searched through the living area and kitchen without finding anything, and then climbed the stairs to look in the two spare bedrooms. There was only Jack's bedroom left.

Callie hesitated with her hand at the door. Why didn't she just wait for Jack and ask him to his face? But she had come this far, she argued with herself. It was silly not to finish what she had started.

Pushing open the door, she went in. The room was furnished in the same simple style as the rest of the villa, with rough white walls and dark wooden chests. A huge bed dominated the room. She and Jack could have been in it now if Spiro hadn't arrived, thought Callie with a surge of resentment. If it was important enough to drag Jack away from her kisses, it was important enough for her to know about.

The package was in the first chest she opened. Would it prove to be a Pandora's box? It was not a comfortable thought and Callie brushed it aside and lifted the heavy lid. Wrapped in sacking, the package lay on top of some linen.

Callie lifted it out carefully and sat back on her heels to open it. The sacking fell aside to reveal a boy carved in stone. He wasn't quite the same as the one Jack had shown her that afternoon, but they were clearly meant to go together. This boy's head was turned slightly as if he was watching, but he had the same untroubled stare and the same secret smile. He was obviously in on the joke. Callie stared down at the smooth perfect lines and her eyes stung with tears.

Was all Jack had told her a lie? Had he made love to her to ensure her silence? Had everything that had happened between them that day been a lie, too?

Very gently she laid the little statue back where she had found it and closed the chest. Then she went slowly downstairs and finished clearing the table. She would wait for Jack to come back and she would ask him outright.

But Jack didn't come back, or at least not until long after Callie had succumbed to exhaustion and crawled into bed, and when she awoke to the sunlight striping the walls through the shutters her suspicions of the night before seemed preposterous.

She squirmed with embarrassment beneath the sheet. How could she have gone through his things like that, just because she was feeling peeved at being left alone? She had been tired and overwrought after such an emotional day, that was all. How nearly she had jeopardised everything by making wild accusations to Jack!

Still, she thought as she dressed that perhaps she should confess that she had been snooping. She pulled on a loose cotton dress and went to find Jack.

He was scribbling a note, but he looked up as she appeared and his face lightened. 'Calypso! At last! I was just writing you a note.'

As always, Callie's heart soared at the sight of him and his kiss put the last of her doubts to flight.

'Are you going out?' she asked when he put her down, flushed and laughing from a comprehensive greeting. She had forgotten all about the package. All that mattered was his arms about her and the warmth of his kiss.

'I was going to get some fresh fish from the port, to cook you a special dinner,' Jack said, tearing up the note. 'Why don't you come with me? You can have breakfast at the taverna.'

She was helpless against his smile. 'All right. I'll get my hat.'

They walked down the track together and the white dust rose up and settled on their shoes.

'What time did you get in?' Callie asked.

'About one.' He glanced down at her face. As it was shaded by the brim of her straw hat, it was difficult to read her expression. 'You were sound asleep, so I didn't wake you, though I was strongly tempted!'

'Did . . . was everything all right?'

Jack looked grave. 'No, not really.'

'Can't you tell me about it?'

'Not yet. But I'll tell you everything tonight. Can you wait till then?'

Callie's eyes were brilliant with relief at not having to admit how suspicious she had been. Jack would tell her everything tonight, and everything would be all right.

'I can wait,' she said.

As they rounded the last bend into the port they saw a line of familiar yachts clustered along the quayside.

'So they were heading here!' Callie said, pointing at them.

'Looks like it. They've usually moved on by this time in the morning, though.' There was a slight frown between Jack's brows. 'I wonder what they're up to.'

Most of the yachts had people sunning themselves on the decks or hanging washing along the rigging. Marcus and Nikki were sitting together outside the taverna, inspecting Nikki's bandaged foot, which lay on a chair between them.

'Yoo-hoo!' Nikki beckoned them over. 'You've discovered us in our hour of disaster!'

'What have you done to your foot?' Jack asked, smiling at her with what Callie thought was unnecessary warmth and nodding briefly at Marcus.

Marcus's nod in return was no more enthusiastic, but his face lit up as he turned to Callie with a welcoming smile. 'Hi, there!' Reaching out, he gave her a quick hug, and, although Callie was surprised, she didn't object. She just thought that Marcus was being particularly friendly, until she happened to glance at Jack in time to see his quick frown. He didn't have any business looking jealous after he'd looked so pleased to see Nikki, she thought with a pinch of resentment, and perversely returned Marcus's greeting effusively.

'You haven't met Nikki before, have you?' Marcus said and introduced the two girls, although neither looked particularly delighted. Whenever she saw Nikki, Callie was conscious of how attractive the other girl was, and she noticed now that the green eyes were hostile as they rested on her. Nikki had evidently not been pleased to see Callie walking so close to Jack.

'What *have* you done, Nikki?' Jack asked, unaware of the unspoken antagonism between the girls.

'I've twisted my ankle,' Nikki explained gaily, tossing back her blonde hair with her hand and turning to him in a way that subtly excluded Callie. 'Honestly, I'm such a clot! I was just running along to tell the Jenkinsons about the barbecue tonight, when I caught my foot in one of the ropes. Talk about clumsy!' She gave a merry laugh that grated up and down Callie's spine. 'They used to call me the jinx at the chalet last winter!'

'It must be sore,' Callie said stiffly, feeling that some comment was called for.

'I'm trying to keep it propped up, but it's a bit difficult on a boat. People keep knocking into it, and then of course it's absolute agony!' Nikki fluttered her eyelashes at Jack, and, to Callie's disgust, he made suitably sympathetic noises. She couldn't imagine Nikki's foot was *that* bad. It wasn't as if she'd broken her leg.

'We were just discussing whether it made sense for Nikki to stay here for a few days,' Marcus put in. He looked relaxed and friendly, and Callie wondered if she had imagined the hard look in his eyes when he had greeted Jack. 'I could take the group off round the other islands and then come back and pick her up when her ankle's a bit less tender.'

'It's such a nuisance,' Nikki sighed. 'It's so important to have someone to get the group together at the beginning too!'

'I'm sure I can struggle by without you,' Marcus said with a grin. 'The main thing is for your ankle to recover. We don't want you limping around all summer!'

Callie thought what a considerate colleague he was. She couldn't understand how Jack could so misjudge him, and yet be taken in by Nikki's blatant flirtation.

'It's going to be awful waving you all off,' Nikki was saying, and then, with a glance at Jack, 'I hate being on my own! You'll be around to keep my spirits up, won't you, Jack?'

'Of course,' he said promptly, and Nikki preened herself.

'Maybe it won't be so bad staying behind after all,' she murmured with another provocative look.

Callie realised that her fists were clenched, and she stared down at the plastic tablecloth, unable to watch how Jack reacted. In the face of Nikki's vivacious personality and glowing looks, she felt pale and uninteresting. The confidence that yesterday's happiness had given her had evaporated in the face of Jack's obvious interest in Nikki, leaving her vulnerable and dismayed.

Had she read too much into Jack's lovemaking yesterday? She had had no doubts at the time, but somehow it didn't seem so obvious with Nikki there. Was it really likely that Jack would prefer her quiet dreaminess to Nikki's sense of fun? 'Nikki has a career in life,' he had said admiringly. Jack was like that too, Callie thought dismally.

It was with a dull sense of inevitability that she saw Jack lean towards Nikki. 'Come and stay at the villa,' he invited her. 'We can look after you for a few days.'

So much for the cosy dinner for two he had promised her, Callie thought bitterly. So much for explanations! Nothing important could be discussed with Nikki sitting there, tossing her hair about and demanding all Jack's willing attention. Sick disappointment settled like a stone in her heart.

'Stay with you?' Nikki made a show of demurring, but she was clearly delighted. 'Wouldn't I be an awful lot of trouble?'

'Of course not,' said Jack, without even glancing at Callie. 'We'd love to have you. It would be fun.'

'Oh, Jack, could I really? That would be *marvellous*! You *are* kind! It would solve all our problems, wouldn't it, Marcus?'

'It would indeed!'

Nikki laid her hand on Jack's arm. 'I can't wait! I'm almost glad I twisted my ankle now!' Her green eyes flickered to Callie, who was concentrating on keeping her expression carefully blank. 'I've got a brilliant idea!' she cried, as if struck by a sudden thought. 'Why doesn't Callie take my place for a few days, Marcus? You've been going on about taking her out for a trip.'

Appalled, Callie glanced at Jack. His dark brows were drawn together, but Marcus took up Nikki's suggestion with enthusiasm.

'Of course! Callie, you did say you'd like to come exploring, didn't you?' Jack's frown deepened, and before Callie had a chance to reply Marcus had carried on. 'You can have Nikki's berth, and we can have the boat to ourselves. I don't see why Jack and Nikki should have all the fun!'

He thought they wanted to be alone too, Callie thought miserably.

Jack was looking thunderous. 'You really need to work on your illustrations, don't you, Callie, before you can take any time off?' he said pointedly.

'Oh, but she might not get another chance to see the other islands!' cried Nikki, obviously desperate to get rid of Callie and have Jack to herself.

Callie hesitated. She didn't want to leave Nikki a clear field with Jack, but what right did he have to be so dog-in-the-manger? He was the one who had invited Nikki, after all, and he wouldn't have asked her if he didn't want to be alone with her.

Where did that leave *her*?

'Come on, Callie!' Marcus said persuasively. 'You'll have much more fun than playing gooseberry to these two.'

'You can't do any work on a boat,' Jack protested.

'I can take my sketchbook with me.' Too hurt and jealous to think clearly, Callie made up her mind. 'You're the one always telling me not to hesitate when I'm offered a chance to have some fun!' Her grey eyes clashed defiantly with Jack's angry blue ones before she turned to Marcus. 'Thanks. I'd love to come!'

'Great!' Marcus leapt to his feet. 'I'll go and get your bag, Nikki, and warn the group that we can leave in about an hour. Is that enough time for you to get ready, Callie?'

She nodded drearily. What had she done?

She was too proud to back out, particularly when Nikki made such a performance of limping that Jack gave in and carried her up the track to the villa while Callie was forced to carry her bag.

'Oh, you are sweet!' cried Nikki.

Callie had never felt less sweet in her life. She and Jack barely exchanged a word on the way back to the villa, although Nikki kept up a ceaseless flow of chatter. He was charming to Nikki, teasing her and making her giggle complacently, but whenever he looked at Callie the blue eyes were hard and unsmiling and the laughing mouth was set in a grim line.

Well, it was all his fault, Callie reminded herself crossly. If he hadn't been so keen to have Nice Nikki to stay, she would never have accepted Marcus's invitation. Let him hold Nikki against his chest, let Nikki wind her arms about his neck. Let him cook his special dinner for two for Nikki. See if she cared!

CHAPTER EIGHT

BACK at the villa, Callie threw some clothes into a bag, terrified that Jack would come in and try to persuade her not to go. She knew that, if he touched her once, she was lost. But he was busy ensconcing Nikki on the terrace, and only caught Callie as she was heading for the door.

'Calypso! Wait!' He was standing at the foot of the stairs, looking up at her, his face dark with displeasure. 'Look, I can explain...'

Callie clutched her bag protectively to her chest. 'You've waited this long to explain everything, Jack. What difference is a few more days going to make?'

'What the hell do you mean by that?'

'I don't know who you are or what you're doing here. Why are you so secretive about everything?'

'I said I was going to tell you tonight!'

'You've made other plans for tonight now, haven't you?' said Callie bitterly. 'I don't mind. I said I could wait.'

Jack's jaw worked furiously. 'I don't trust Marcus,' he warned.

'Well, I trust him a lot more than I trust *you*! At least he's never lied to me!'

'I haven't lied to you!'

'Maybe not, but you've never told me the whole truth either, have you, Jack?'

'Look, Calypso——' Jack began to start up the stairs towards her, but at that moment Nikki called merrily through from the terrace.

'What an *amazing* view!'

'You'd better go and *be nice* to your guest!' Callie said waspishly. 'You know how nice you can be when you try!'

'Calypso!' Jack was taking the stairs two at a time and she turned in desperation to the door.

'I've got to go. Marcus will be waiting!' She struggled frantically with the door, but at last it opened and she slammed it behind her before running down the track towards the port, tears streaming down her face.

Jack didn't follow her any further. Callie stumbled to a halt and glanced back, but the door was still firmly closed, shutting her out. He wasn't that desperate to explain.

Closing her heart, she turned and ran on down to the port. She stopped once to wipe away her tears, and to catch her breath before she had to face a lot of strangers, but to her relief most of the yachts were using their motors to leave the port by the time she arrived. Fortunately, Marcus was shouting last-minute instructions at the remaining few and was too busy to notice her reddened eyes.

'At last!' he said, turning to her with a smile as the last yachts got under way. 'They're all taking the picturesque route to our meeting point, so we've got plenty of time. I usually follow on behind, just in case anyone's having any problems.'

He took Callie's bag and helped her on to the boat. 'Welcome aboard! This has all worked out perfectly, hasn't it? I knew Nikki was angling to stay at the villa, but, stupidly, I hadn't thought about you taking her place until she suggested it. This way it suits everybody. She and Jack get to be alone, and as you don't get on with Jack anyway I imagine you'll be glad of a chance to leave them to get on with it. And, of course, I get your company for a few days,' he added gallantly. 'It couldn't be better, could it?'

'No,' said Callie dismally, lacerated by jealousy at the thought of Jack and Nikki 'getting on with it'. She had given Marcus the impression that she didn't like Jack when she had met him on Ilonika, so it wasn't really his fault that she wanted to die.

Why, why, why had she agreed to come? As the sails unfurled and a perfect breeze sent them scudding through the glittering water, all she could think about was Jack—Jack and Nikki.

He would have to carry her up to bed. Her ankle probably wasn't twisted at all, Callie decided morosely. It was probably just a ruse to get Jack to lift her in his powerful arms. Callie could just imagine Nikki shaking back her blonde hair appealingly as she slipped her arms around his neck. How could Jack resist that voluptuously sun-streaked beauty? Nikki was so nice and such fun. A girl who liked to have a good time, he had said. Not like shy, boring, uptight Calypso. Nikki would never hesitate if she was offered excitement and adventure.

Callie stared blindly at the waves, absorbed in her thoughts, her delicate profile etched against the azure sky, until Marcus interrupted her thoughts.

'You're such a funny, dreamy little thing,' he said with some amusement. 'No wonder you didn't get on with Jack. He's so boisterous, isn't he?'

Callie thought about the slow delight of Jack's kisses, the way he smiled against her skin.

'Not always.'

Suddenly she realised that Marcus had pulled down the sails and was letting down the anchor. 'Are we there already?'

'No, but, as I said, we've plenty of time. I thought we might do a little exploring in the inflatable. I'm always on the look-out for good places to have a barbecue and I'm sure I spotted a hidden bay round here the other day. Might be a good place to go diving, too. Some of the caves round here are quite spectacular.'

Caves? Callie's head jerked round, remembering the grotto. To her horror, she realised that they were anchored in the bay overlooked by the Villa Oleander, just outside the beach she and Jack had visited yesterday. There was the villa in the distance, half hidden by the tangle of lemon trees and bougainvillaea. Her heart twisted with longing. If only she were there now! She didn't want Marcus to find the beach. She didn't want anyone to find it. It belonged to her, and Jack. And what if Marcus found the grotto? Callie went cold at the very thought.

She cleared her throat. 'Oh, I know the bay you mean,' she said, desperate to discourage him. 'It's not much of a beach. I wouldn't think it would be suitable for barbecues.'

'You didn't see any signs of caves, then? I've done quite a bit of diving around this area and the cliffs seem to be riddled with them.'

'I didn't notice anything,' Callie said doggedly, avoiding his eye. 'It was all a bit dull.' *Dull*? That magical beach? Surely Marcus could read the lie emblazoned on her forehead?

Marcus was undeterred. 'We might as well have a look, since we're here,' he said cheerfully.

There was nothing for it but to climb down into the inflatable tender that was tied to the back of the boat and let Marcus cast off. There was no way he could miss the beach from here, she thought with a sinking heart, but still she found herself hoping against hope that he wouldn't spot the narrow entrance.

He found it almost immediately. The inflatable ground against the beach and she stepped out on to the sand. This was where she and Jack had lain yesterday. This was where his body had taken her to the heart-stopping limits of rapture. This was where he had shown her what loving could be.

Callie ached with remembered desire. Wrenching her eyes away from the shoreline, she stared desperately at the cliffs, but images from yesterday were burning into her mind and all she could see was Jack's hand on her thigh, his lips at her breast.

Marcus didn't appear to notice her abstraction. He was pacing the beach like a surveyor, his eyes checking the height of the cliffs and the width of the entrance to the little bay.

Callie held her breath as he neared the rocky outcrop that hid the crevice, but he didn't think to look behind it and she sighed with relief as he came back towards her.

'Nice place,' he said, and she thought he looked at her rather intently as if wondering what she would say.

Remembering that she had told him it wasn't much of a beach, Callie bit her lip. 'It's nicer than I remembered,' she said lamely.

'Not much potential for diving, though,' Marcus went on, still watching her closely. 'Odd. I expected there would be lots of little caves leading off an inlet like this. Still, it's a nice sheltered place for a barbecue.'

Callie thought of endless groups frolicking on the beach, shattering the peace and poking among the rocks. Sooner or later someone would be bound to find the grotto. She cast around wildly for some way to discourage Marcus.

'The beach is rather small for a big group, isn't it?' she tried, and Marcus studied her thoughtfully.

She was relieved when he looked away. 'Perhaps you're right. We'd have trouble getting the boats through that gap anyway. Too many rocks about.'

At last he was ready to leave. Callie couldn't wait to get away. The empty beach seemed to mock her with memories, and she was terrified that Marcus would decide that the boats could reach the bay after all.

'Aren't you glad you came?' Marcus asked as the inflatable bounced over the waves. 'This is much more fun than slaving away over your sketchbook! It seems like a good group too, so we should have some crack at the barbecue tonight. You'll have a good time.'

Callie's eyes rested on the villa. What were Jack and Nikki doing now? They wouldn't mind missing out on a barbecue when they could have the night to themselves. The thought brought up her chin.

'I'm sure I will,' she said with an over-bright smile.

The next few days were the most miserable of her life. The holiday-makers in the group were, as Marcus had said, friendly and determined to enjoy themselves. Callie smiled and laughed until she thought her face would crack with the effort, but her jaw ached continuously from fighting back the tears. All she wanted was to get back to Jack.

Marcus was charming and attentive but he wasn't Jack. She knew that, if she hadn't been so nervous about his discovering the grotto, she would never have felt the vague unease about him on the beach.

He certainly never gave her any reason to distrust him. He was just open and friendly and ... *normal.* Sometimes Callie would look at his pleasant face and reassuringly steady brown eyes and feel guilty that she didn't appreciate all his efforts to entertain her. It wasn't his fault that he didn't have wickedly glinting blue eyes or a smile to set her heart lurching madly.

She wished she hadn't made such a scene before she left. She should have bitten her tongue and welcomed Nikki instead of storming off and leaving her alone with Jack. He was worth fighting for.

Callie tortured herself by wondering what they were doing. Were they laughing together? Was he kissing her? Were they lying on the beach or rolling in the waves? She tried to sketch some seascapes, but ended up drawing Jack obsessively. She felt as if she could draw every crease around his eyes, every angle of his face, and she would look down at the completed drawing and her body would throb with need of him.

It felt like an eternity before the flotilla headed back into Pikos in the late-afternoon light. Callie's heart soared as the familiar cluster of houses came into sight. They had sailed among the stark beauty of the islands, and anchored in bays so lovely that no amount of travel agent's prose could do them justice, but none of it had the power to lift her spirits. They were all just places without Jack, and, for all the inspiration she had found, she might just as well have been drifting around the grimmest of industrial conurbations.

Marcus and the group all congratulated themselves that she had had a wonderful time; she must be a better actress than she had ever suspected, Callie thought as she thanked Marcus again and waved goodbye before setting off up the track to oust Nikki from her place on the terrace.

There was a shout as she rounded the bend, and she stopped in surprise. Spiro was ambling up the hill after her, waving something in his hand.

What did *he* want? Callie scowled at him, convinced that he was responsible for leading Jack into some shady business, but as he came closer she saw that he was holding some letters. He was trying to tell her something, pointing out to sea, and at last she spotted the ferry just disappearing over the horizon.

'The letters have just arrived on the ferry?' she hazarded.

Spiro nodded, although she was sure he didn't understand any more English than she did Greek. He thrust the letters into her hand and she gathered that she would save him a walk if she would take them to the villa.

'OK, I'll take them.'

Spiro smiled, a disconcertingly charming smile, and raised a hand in farewell before strolling back to the harbour.

Glancing through the letters, Callie saw that they were all for Garth Havelock except for one. She turned it over. It was for her, from Antonia. Callie raised her brows. It wasn't like Antonia to write back so quickly! She hesitated, about to open it, and then changed her mind. She wanted to see Jack. There would be plenty of time to read Antonia's letter later.

Suddenly she was desperate to see Jack. What if he'd gone? Unreasoning panic seized her and she stuffed the letters into her pocket and practically ran up the hill.

She burst into the villa to find Jack and Nikki lounging on the long white sofas. They looked very comfortable together, and fresh doubt washed over her.

'Calypso.' Jack got slowly to his feet to look up at her standing at the top of the stairs. For a moment she thought she saw a blaze of welcome in his eyes, and then his face took on a shuttered look. 'We were expecting you.' He made it sound almost sinister and a chill touched Callie's heart.

'We watched the boats go round the headland,' Nikki explained, reluctantly gathering up her bags. 'I'd better go down, I suppose, or Marcus will be champing at the bit to get on. Did you have a good time?'

'Great,' lied Callie, coming down the stairs.

'I told Jack you'd enjoy yourself,' Nikki said complacently. 'It's such fun, and Marcus is a star, isn't he?'

'Yes, he is. He's very nice.' Callie was itching for Nikki to go.

She could see Jack mouthing 'He's very nice' behind Nikki's back in unkind imitation. He obviously hadn't forgiven her for going off with Marcus.

At last Nikki was ready. Jack saw her to the door for a noisy and protracted farewell.

Callie didn't want to know whether Nikki kissed him goodbye or not. She wandered out on to the terrace to wait for Jack, wondering why he had looked quite so boot-faced when he had seen her. She had spent so long dreaming of what she would say when she saw him again, but it didn't look as if it was going to be anything like she had imagined.

Was Nikki never going to go? Stupidly nervous, Callie thrust her hands in her pockets to stop them shaking and remembered the letters Spiro had given her. She dropped Garth's on to the table and ripped open Antonia's incuriously, her mind still on Jack. Antonia had written,

Whoops! I really blew it this time, didn't I? But it seemed such a good plan for you to go to the villa while he was away... how was I to know he'd decide not to go to the States after all?

Puzzled, Callie read the first paragraph again. What was Antonia talking about?

I was going to check with Stella about you going, but she was away and her return kept being delayed, so in the end I just took the key. I was sure there wouldn't be a problem because I'd booked his flight to Los Angeles myself. I didn't tell you I hadn't actually checked because I could see you were on the verge of sloping back to boring old Neil as it was.

A cold feeling was beginning to trickle down Callie's spine.

Anyway, it all seems to have worked out all right. I nearly died when he rang me from Ilonika just after you'd arrived, but he was absolutely charming about it. He seemed quite taken with you! Just as well, as Stella was furious with me until he calmed her down and told her he'd always wanted a nymph to blow in off the sea. He does have some funny ideas, doesn't he? Still, I suppose, since you've read all his books, you know what he's talking about. I must read them one day!

Callie sat down abruptly at the table. Antonia's scrawl seemed to waver in the bright sunlight and she blinked hard to focus as she turned the page with shaking hands.

We had a good giggle when your card arrived. I bet you felt a fool when you realised! He's a bit paranoid about his privacy, as you know. We're not allowed to tell anyone his real name, so I couldn't have told you even if I'd thought it was necessary. Do you know why he decided to stay after all? Stella just said that he'd told her that something important had come up. It took me ages to cancel all his bookings, too.

You must be in heaven, having your hero there as well, so I won't ask if you're having a good time! He's not at all as you'd expect, is he? Bet you're grateful to me now! Tons of love, Antonia.

Grateful! The letter dropped from Callie's nerveless hands and she leant her elbows on the table, pressing the heels of her hands against her eyes in despair.

What a fool she had been! What a blind, stupid fool! It was all so obvious now. Why hadn't she guessed?

No wonder Jack had been so amused when she sprang to Garth Havelock's defence. What was it she had said? 'He's generous, sensitive and a marvellous writer,' and 'I've always imagined him as my perfect hero.' All that fishing for information about him! Pretending she knew him! How could she have been so stupid?

Callie squeezed her eyes tight, awash with humiliation as she remembered everything she had said and the suspicions she had had about Jack's vague relationship with Garth Havelock.

She had been so certain that she knew what Garth would be like. 'He's not at all as you'd expect, is he?' How right Antonia had been! She had imagined him to be intense and other-worldly, not radiating life and laughter.

Callie's eyes darkened as she thought how much of that laughter must have been at her expense, and she welcomed the anger that flared suddenly, burning away the humiliation. She had wondered once before if everything between them had been a lie, and now she was sure.

She could hear Jack coming down the stairs. Nikki must have gone at last. She was proud of how steady her hands were as they refolded Antonia's letter and slipped it back into the envelope. She didn't look round, even though she knew that Jack was standing in the doorway, watching her.

'Well?' he said eventually. There was no mistaking the hostility in his voice.

'Well what?'

'*Did* you have a good time with Marcus? You were gone long enough!'

'It wasn't up to me to decide when we came back. I had to fit in with the flotilla's plans.' Callie's back was rigid. 'Anyway, it didn't look as if you and Nikki missed me very much. She could hardly bear to leave!'

Jack ignored that. 'So what did you and Marcus get up to? Must have been cosy sharing a boat— or was it a berth? Nikki tells me he's quite a lad. A different girl every trip.'

'Marcus isn't like that!'

'Oh, no, I forgot.' Jack prowled over to the terrace wall. 'He's nice and reliable, just like your precious Neil. I suppose you thought that, since you'd had your bit of excitement, you'd revert back to type!'

'Nothing happened between Marcus and me!' Callie leapt to her feet, her eyes blazing. 'We sailed from island to island and Marcus was charming, but that's all.'

'No romantic little trips, just the two of you on the beach?'

'No!'

'Liar!' He strode towards her, grabbing her arms and shaking her. 'You went straight from here to our beach. Nikki recognised the boat and we watched you both climb into the inflatable and head right for the entrance. Did you tell Marcus what a nice little place you'd found, just right for a little love in the afternoon? Did you show him the grotto?' He shook her again. 'Did you?'

Callie wrenched herself free. 'No, I didn't show him your rotten grotto! I tried to persuade him the beach wasn't worth seeing, but he'd caught a glimpse and was determined to have a look. I didn't have much choice but to go along.'

'What did you do while you were there?'

'Nothing.'

'You must have done something!'

I thought about you, she wanted to cry. I thought about you and how happy we had been. Instead she said, 'I just sat on the beach, and Marcus had a look around. And, before you ask, no, he didn't find the crevice.'

'And then what?'

'Then he decided it wasn't a suitable place for a barbecue and we left. If you and Nikki had still been spying on us you'd have seen that we went back to the boat almost immediately.'

She rubbed her arms as Jack turned and went back to lean on the wall. 'Look, what is all this? Why the interrogation?'

'Someone's been in the grotto,' he said heavily.

'How do you know?'

'They've started to lift the mosaic.'

'*What*?' Callie stared at him in horror. 'Is it badly damaged?'

'It's been expertly done, and it's not an easy job. Someone knows what they're doing. My guess is that they've taken a small piece to get a valuation on the black market.'

'But…' Callie stopped. 'Surely you don't suspect Marcus of being involved?'

'Who else?'

'It might be anybody,' she protested. 'What about Spiro? He's not exactly the picture of innocence!'

'You're so naïve, Calypso! Do you really think all villains look shifty and wear hats pulled down over their eyes? It was Spiro who found the damage and came to me.'

'Why didn't he go the police?'

'Because the authorities don't know anything about the grotto,' Jack said impatiently. 'I told you there was a tacit agreement among the islanders to keep it quiet and they're not likely to go running to the police now. We just need to catch these people at it and deal with them ourselves.'

'They might be dangerous,' Callie said, appalled, and Jack turned with a smile that didn't reach his eyes.

'I can be dangerous too.'

Callie remembered what Marcus had said about Jack—'he's a dangerous man'—and she shivered.

'What makes you think it's Marcus?'

Jack shrugged. 'I don't *know* it's him. It's just a feeling. His visits are a bit too convenient. I didn't tell you before, but one or two of the smaller bowls and statues have gone missing recently—only since he started coming to the island. What better place to hide them than on the boats sailing innocently around the islands? It would be easy for him to get the stuff out. He'd just have to ask someone in the group to post a present to his mother when they got back to England or something like that.'

'But Marcus has been with me over the last few days,' Callie pointed out. 'He couldn't have had anything to do with the mosaic.'

'Has he been with you twenty-four hours a day?' Jack asked.

'Well, no...' Callie thought about the times she had told Marcus she wanted to do some drawings while he went off in the boat. All she had really wanted to do was sit and think about Jack. 'He did go off diving once or twice, and one night he went fishing.'

'And you believed him, I suppose.'

'I believed you when you said *you* were going fishing,' she said angrily. 'Why should I believe you more than him?'

Jack's face was set in hard lines. 'I should never have let you go off with him! I *told* you I didn't trust him!'

'You told me lots of things, Jack,' Callie said, bitterness edging her voice. 'And now I don't believe any of them.'

A muscle jumped in Jack's cheek. 'Funny that you're so quick to believe Marcus instead of me! I thought you trusted me. We made love, Calypso. Didn't that afternoon mean anything to you? Didn't you know me well enough after that to trust me, instead of jumping to conclusions about Nikki?'

He made as if to start towards her, but Callie hardly noticed. 'You're a fine one to talk about trusting, Jack! How dare you accuse me of not trusting you when you didn't even trust me enough to tell me your name?' Snatching up the letters addressed to Garth Havelock, she threw them at Jack's feet. 'Here, these are for you!'

Jack bent to pick up the letters. He looked at the name, and then at Callie.

'Ah,' he said slowly, and dropped the letters back on to the table.

There was a short silence, broken by Callie.

'You *are* Garth Havelock?'

'How did you find out?'

'Antonia told me—or, rather, she assumed I knew. I gather you've all had a good laugh at my expense. What a good joke to let me carry on thinking you were two different people! You must have laughed yourself silly!'

'It wasn't like that,' said Jack, taking a step towards her, but she backed away behind the table.

'Wasn't it? What *was* it like, Jack—or should I say Garth? Which one is the real you?'

'You know the real me,' he said quietly.

'Do I? It doesn't seem like it right now.' To her fury, Callie found that she was crying, and she turned her back on him, wiping her face with the backs of her hands. 'I thought I knew everything about you that mattered, but I didn't know then that everything you told me was a lie!'

CHAPTER NINE

'IT WASN'T a lie,' Jack said angrily. 'My name is Jack Kingsley, just as I told you. Garth Havelock is just a pseudonym. He doesn't exist. There's just me, and I never pretended to be anything other than what I am. *You* were the one who made up a character for Garth, but you did it without any help from me! It was just your wishful thinking.'

'You talked about him as if he were a real person,' Callie accused him on a sob. 'You let me make a real fool of myself, didn't you? I told you all about how marvellous I thought you were, and all the time you were sitting there sniggering to yourself!'

Jack had followed her round the table, and she was forced to retreat into the corner of the terrace, ducking beneath the overhanging branches of the lemon tree.

'All right!' he shouted. 'I *was* amused. You were so determined to believe what you wanted! But I was always going to tell you. It was just difficult to find the right moment. I was afraid you would either refuse to believe me or that you'd make just the kind of fuss you're making now!'

'Don't patronise me, Jack!' Callie flared, turning her back on him. 'I don't suppose it occurred to you to wonder how I might feel at finding out that you were someone completely different? You just didn't want me to be unreasonable and make a fuss! What am I expected to do? Smile and say ''That's all right, Jack, I don't mind if you couldn't be bothered to tell me who you were''?'

'I'm not someone different. That's what I'm trying to tell you!' Jack sounded exasperated. 'I'm sorry if you feel humiliated now, but you would have felt the same whenever you found out.'

'It wouldn't have been so bad if you'd told me yourself!'

'I *was* going to tell you. I'd just worked myself up to a confession that night when Spiro interrupted us.' Jack paused, looking at Callie's tense spine and miserably hunched shoulders, and when he spoke again the anger was gone from his voice. 'You remember that night, don't you, Calypso? You sat on my lap and kissed me and told me you didn't care about Garth, you just wanted to be with me. I'm the same person I was then. Nothing's changed.'

Callie swung round, her huge grey eyes still shimmering with tears. 'Hasn't it? Don't you think that your few days with Nikki might have changed things a bit? Did I bore you that quickly? You couldn't wait to get her back here!'

'Just as you couldn't wait to go off with your precious Marcus!'

'I didn't have much choice. It was pretty obvious I wasn't wanted here!'

'That's not true,' Jack said, tight-lipped. 'I didn't want you to go. I wanted you to stay.'

'It didn't seem that way to me,' said Callie bitterly.

He sighed. 'Look, I felt sorry for Nikki, but there were other reasons why I wanted to get her on her own.'

'I can imagine what *they* were!'

'Not what you're thinking.' Jack's face darkened. 'Obviously there's no point in trying to convince you at the moment. You'll just have to believe me when I say that Nikki's stay was completely innocent.'

'Oh, come on, Jack! She was all over you! I'm not that naïve.'

'In other words, you don't trust me,' he said flatly.

'You haven't given me any reason to trust you.'

'No?' Brushing aside the branch, Jack advanced on her until she was trapped against the corner of the terrace. 'What about the other afternoon? What about *this*?' he asked, and with a smothered exclamation jerked her into his arms.

It was a long, hard, angry kiss, and Callie was breathless and shaken by the time he let her go. She stared up at him with dazed eyes.

'No wonder you've got such a lousy track record with men,' Jack said contemptuously. 'You won't trust anyone. I don't think you even trust yourself. You see people as you want to see them, not as they are, and then feel hurt when they don't behave as you expected. You wanted Garth Havelock to be some romantic hero, and he turned out to be me instead. Tough luck. You can take me as I am, or not at all, and taking me means trusting me. If you can't do that, you'd better run back to Neil after all.'

Turning abruptly, he strode across the terrace to the glass doors.

Callie found her voice. 'Wh-where are you going?'

'To the taverna. I'll leave you to work things out for yourself.'

Lying on her bed that night, Callie watched the patterns the moonlight made on the floor and thought about what Jack had said. Humiliation and jealousy had made her angry, but the calm, quiet night made everything seem different. He was right. Did it really matter that he was Garth Havelock? Surely all that mattered was the way he was? Still, it was impossible not to feel that he had held back a vital part of himself. Knowing that the man she loved had written those books had turned him suddenly into a stranger.

But she still loved him. Even when she was shouting and accusing and pretending to hate him, all she had wanted was for him to take her into his arms again. Had she ruined everything by not trusting him as he wanted? *Could* she trust him as he wanted?

She couldn't sleep. Eventually she gave up trying and went back to sit on the terrace, hoping that the soothing murmur of the sea would stop the thoughts whirling around her brain, but it was no good. The night was too full of memories.

The fragrance of the lemon trees reminded her achingly of how Jack had pulled her on to his lap and kissed her as if he loved her. He had never said so. Why should he? She had made such an idiot of herself. No wonder he treated her like a silly child. And yet that afternoon on the beach...he had treated her as a woman then.

Callie looked across the bay, remembering, and suddenly sat up straighter. Had that been the flash of a torch over there? She stared until her eyes began to ache. Perhaps she had imagined it? No, there it was again.

Someone was on the beach.

If they were there in the darkness it could only mean that they were stealing from the grotto. Callie jumped to her feet and then stood, irresolute. How was she going to stop them? She could run down to the taverna and try to find Jack, but that might lose valuable time. The thieves might be long gone by the time they got there.

Another, worse thought crossed her mind.

What if it *was* Jack?

The statue lying in the chest upstairs nagged at her mind. Why had he hidden it there?

Callie made up her mind. She would go to the beach herself. If it was Jack, at least she would know. If it was someone else, she would just have to stop them herself.

Running back up the stairs, she changed quickly into a dark shirt and pulled on a pair of jeans before slipping quietly out of the house.

There was a clear moon, hidden every now and then by drifting clouds. It made it difficult to see the path until her eyes adjusted to the darkness, and she was forced to feel her way with agonising slowness through the more overgrown parts. On the wider sections, when the moon emerged from behind a cloud to light her way, she ran as fast as she dared, trying not to think about how near the cliff edge was.

Once she stumbled and fell heavily. Badly winded, she lay with her heart hammering against her ribs. Her hands were badly grazed and her face and arms scratched by the undergrowth, and for a long moment she thought she would be too frightened ever to move again.

It had been stupid to come alone, but it was too late now. Having got this far, she would have to go on. Shakily Callie got to her feet and brushed down her jeans. She took the next section a little more slowly, but then she began to panic about missing the thieves altogether and broke into a run again.

She had forgotten how far it was. By the time she reached the top of the cliff she was staggering with exhaustion, and she hung her head to her knees to try and get her breath back.

Down on the beach, a light flashed again.

Callie crept nearer to the edge of the cliff and peered over. A boat was pulled up on to the beach, and beside it she could see the dark figures of two men conferring together. As she watched they turned and headed for the crevice hidden behind the rocky outcrop. That meant it couldn't be Marcus. He hadn't known it was there.

When they had disappeared Callie began to pick her way down the steep slope as quietly as she could. Last time she had had Jack's hand to catch her if she slipped.

Don't think about Jack, she told herself crossly. Just think about getting safely down this path.

Once on the beach, she crouched behind a rock and wondered what she should do next. All she wanted to do was to scrabble back up the cliff, run back to the villa and hide herself under the bed-clothes, but a stern inner voice told her she was being silly.

You don't have to confront them. Just see who it is, and then you can go and find Jack, she decided, allowing herself a moment to fantasise about how grateful he would be to her for catching the thieves red-handed. Perhaps it would make up for her childish fury.

Stiffening her spine resolutely, Callie straightened cautiously and squinted over the rock, only to duck down again in a panic. A fine secret agent she'd make!

A man had emerged from the crevice and was carrying something towards the boat, his feet making no sound on the soft sand. Very, very carefully Callie inched herself round to see if she could get a look at his face. The moon was hidden behind a cloud, but, just when she was beginning to despair, it burst through, illuminating the man's face as he lifted his head and looked around him nervously.

It wasn't Jack.

That was all Callie could think as she sank back into her hiding-place, dizzy with relief. It wasn't Jack and it wasn't Marcus. It wasn't anyone she knew, although she was sure she had seen him somewhere before...where was it? She shook her head. It would come back to her. In the meantime, she couldn't wait to tell Jack how wrong he had been about Marcus!

Another peep round the rock showed her that the man was heading back to the grotto. That would give her time to have a quick look in the boat before either of them reappeared. She waited until he was out of sight, then ran swiftly down the beach to the inflatable.

A tiny wave broke over her feet, but she barely noticed the cold water seeping into her canvas shoes as she bent over the boat. Diving equipment was piled up at one end, but in the middle lay a box covered with sacking. Callie tugged it aside and began to scrabble through the packing straw. They were being careful not to damage anything as they moved it.

Her fingers closed around something smooth and hard and she drew it out of the straw. It was the boy Jack had shown her in the grotto. As Callie stared down at him, a shaft of moonlight fell on his face, still smiling his secretive smile.

It was then that she became angry. Up until now she had been more concerned about Jack than the grotto, but now the reality hit. They were stripping the shrine bare, laying barbarian hands on its treasures, desecrating its peace. How *dared* they? Well, they weren't going to get away with it, not if she could help it!

Callie glanced down at the box again. It was too heavy for her to carry on her own. Somehow she must keep them here until she could get help, but she could hardly tackle two men on her own. She had to immobilise the boat, but how? She didn't know how to start the engine, let alone do anything clever to sabotage it.

Biting her thumb, she was looking wildly around the boat—there must be *something* she could do!—when another brief burst of moonshine caught a gleam among the diving equipment. A diver's knife! Callie snatched it up and stabbed it into the inflated sides of the boat. The rubber was tougher than she had thought, but eventually she managed to make a little tear. It didn't seem to be having much effect, so she made a few wild stabs at the other sections too, panicky in case the men should come back. There was no time to waste.

She thought about keeping the knife, but it seemed a little melodramatic and, anyway, she knew that she would never be able to use it against anyone. So she threw it down, grabbed the statue again as proof, and turned to run up the beach towards the shelter of the rocks.

'Where do you think you're going?'

Callie froze, her heart leaping with terror at the menace underlying the quiet voice. Very slowly she turned to the man walking down from the crevice.

'So it *was* you!' she said.

Marcus smiled without humour. 'There doesn't seem much point in denying it now, does there? I suppose your friend Jack Kingsley told you?'

'He suspected you, but I didn't believe him.' Callie shook her head. 'I still can't believe it.'

'You'd better start believing it,' Marcus said coldly and to her horror she saw that he was holding a gun, its snub barrel gleaming evilly in the moonlight. 'What are you doing here?'

'I—I saw some lights from the villa,' Callie said, still gaping at the gun. She couldn't believe this was happening to her. Was pleasant, friendly Marcus really standing there pointing a *gun* at her? 'Jack told me that someone had been taking things from the grotto, so I came to investigate.'

'On your own?'

'Jack's just coming,' Callie lied desperately. If only it were true! 'He went to get help but he'll be here any minute.'

'Not a very good liar, are you, Callie?' Marcus sneered. 'I think you came on your own. Rather a stupid thing to do, wasn't it?'

'Yes,' she admitted. It was true, after all.

'You'd better hand over that, for a start,' Marcus said, nodding at the statue in her hand.

'No!' Callie clutched it to her chest, recovering her anger. 'It doesn't belong to you. You've no right to take these things! They belong to Greece.'

'Nobody's going to miss them,' he said contemptuously.

'Why are you doing this?' she burst out.

'Why do you think? Money, of course. That statue alone is virtually priceless—except that we will accept a price for it in the end. Nothing's beyond price, is it?'

Callie looked at him with disgust. 'Jack told me not to trust you, but I wouldn't listen to him. I told him you were nice. How wrong can you be?'

'Jack?' said Marcus, unmoved. 'Jack Kingsley is a little too busy for his own good. He asks too many questions. I'd hoped Nikki might keep him occupied for a few days, but when she told me what he'd been asking I decided it was time for us to clear out. Pity. If we'd had a bit more time we could have lifted the mosaic. Still,' he glanced at the boat with satisfaction, 'we've enough here to keep us going for a few years.'

'Is Nikki involved in this too?' Callie demanded.

'No, she's the genuine article. She actually likes socialising with the punters!' Marcus gave a short, incredulous laugh. 'Just as well, as she's going to have a lot of explaining to do tomorrow when they find out I've disappeared.'

Callie swallowed. His gun hadn't wavered once. 'Who's that other man?'

'Philippe? He's an archaeologist—a useful person to have around when you're dealing with stuff like this. Lucky for me, he was bored with not finding anything at the site. I'd never have been able to think about tackling the mosaic without him.'

She remembered now where she had seen the Frenchman before. Marcus himself had pointed him out to her on Ilonika. That was when she had been too busy being suspicious of Jack to question the truth of what Marcus said. How naïve she had been! Naïve and stupid and irresponsible. Would she ever be able to face Jack again? Callie looked at the dark shape in Marcus's hand and her stomach churned with fear. Would she see him again at all?

The darkness seemed to press round her as the cold reality of her position hit her. She might never see Jack smile again, never feel the touch of his brown hand. Jack had wanted her to face reality, and now this was it. No one knew she was here and she was defenceless against the ruthless stranger with Marcus's face and Marcus's steady brown eyes. Panic welled up, closing her throat, choking her, and then, incredibly, she saw a shadow move stealthily behind him and disappear behind another rock.

It had been the merest movement, but it was enough to send hope surging through her on a rush of adrenalin. If she could just keep Marcus talking, help might be at hand.

'Who told you about the grotto?' She couldn't believe how calm her voice sounded. 'I can't believe anyone on the island talked about it.'

'Close-mouthed bunch, aren't they? No, Philippe and I found it quite by accident when were were diving one day. We were amazed it hadn't been cleaned out before; someone on the island must know about it.'

The casual cynicism made Callie clench her fists. There was no sign of the shadow. Could she have been mistaken? But no, there it was again.

'It took us a long time to find a way into the grotto that didn't involve taking everything out underwater.' Marcus seemed content to carry on talking, but Callie could tell he was alert for the slightest sound. 'It was all right for one or two pieces, but for a big move like this we needed to get the stuff into a boat. I knew there had to be an entrance somewhere from this beach. I even brought you here especially in the hope that you'd show me. I knew that Jack must have told you something because you were so nervous while we were here, but you wouldn't play, would you? I found it eventually, though.'

Callie hated the complacency in his voice. 'You mustn't take these things, Marcus,' she said desperately.

'It's a pity you decided to poke your nose in to-night, Callie,' Marcus said with a quiet reflectiveness that was terrifying. 'I always liked you, really I did, and I thought you might be quite useful for a while to keep tabs on Jack, but you're a bit of a nuisance now. In fact, you're a very big nuisance. I'm afraid we're going to have to do something about you. Philippe should be here any minute, but first you can give me that statue you're clutching. It won't help you.'

'No.' Callie put it behind her back.

'Come on, don't waste time,' he said impatiently, and jerked the gun. 'This isn't a toy. I don't particularly want to risk a shot yet, but I will.'

Callie's heart thudded painfully. 'No. It's not yours.'

'Don't be stupid, Callie.' Marcus took a step closer, glancing over his shoulder irritably. 'What's Philippe doing in there?'

Terrified that he might have seen the shadow slipping between the rocks towards him, Callie knew that she had to force his attention back to her.

'You won't get away.'

'How are you going to stop us?' jeered Marcus.

'I already have.' Callie looked towards the boat, rejoicing to see that the sides had deflated noticeably. 'I've holed your boat.'

'You little bitch!' After one incredulous look at the boat, Marcus leapt towards her in fury, bringing up his arm for a savage blow.

Callie was knocked to the sand, but the next instant he was brought crashing down by a flying tackle from behind. Dazed, she cowered aside as the two bodies struggled viciously beside her, flinching at the brutal sounds of hand-to-hand fighting.

As she tried to drag herself away her hand hit something cold and metallic, and she clutched at it. Marcus's gun must have been knocked from his hand as he fell.

Callie's knees shook as she staggered to her feet, gun in one hand and statue still held protectively against her with the other, and tried desperately to focus on the men fighting at her feet.

She had the gun. That ought to put her in charge, but all she could do was croak, 'Stop it!' and it was doubtful if they could even hear her. Her hand wavering, she pointed the gun unsteadily down at them, but, even as she realised that there was no way she could be sure of hitting the right man, it was taken roughly from her hand.

'I'll take that,' said Jack.

'Oh, Jack!' Callie sat down abruptly in the sand, too shaken to do anything except cry with relief.

Suddenly the beach seemed to be full of men. Marcus was jerked to his feet, swearing, and his assailant was helped up more gently. As he turned, gingerly rubbing his jaw, she saw that it was Spiro. Spiro, whom she had distrusted from the first, just because of how he looked. Callie looked down at the statue in her hand, ashamed. She would never trust her instincts again.

Jack had handed the gun to a tough-looking man and was talking to him in rapid Greek. The man nodded occasionally, then turned away to talk into a radio. A few minutes later two speed launches with searchlights full on powered through the narrow entrance to the bay.

Callie could only blink at all the activity. Her head ached violently where Marcus had hit her and she was shivering with reaction. She longed to throw herself into Jack's arms, but he was busy supervising the transfer of Marcus and Philippe to one of the launches. There seemed to be some discussion going on, for at length Jack nodded decisively and came across to where Callie was resting her aching head on her knees.

His expression hardened as he looked down at her. 'It's not your evening, is it, Calypso?'

Puzzled, she stared up at him, her eyes enormous in her white face. 'Jack, who are all these people?'

'Police. Sorry if we spoiled your plans.'

'My plans?' Callie echoed stupidly. 'I don't understand.'

Jack pointed to the figure she still held like a talisman. 'Weren't you planning to share the pickings with your nice friend Marcus?'

'No!' she cried, but he interrupted her.

'Oh, don't worry. I've told the police you weren't really involved, just a silly little girl who didn't know what she was doing, and they've agreed to pretend that you weren't here. I hope you're grateful!'

Callie scrambled awkwardly to her feet. 'But Jack, you don't understand!'

'No,' he said heavily. 'I don't understand, but I don't want to hear any more excuses either. I don't know whether you cooked this up when you were with Marcus, or whether it's some kind of childish revenge on me for not telling you about Garth Havelock, and I don't care. I'm going to Athens now, so I'll leave Spiro to relieve you of your booty!'

CHAPTER TEN

TURNING on his heel, Jack strode down towards the boats, leaving Callie stricken and defeated.

'Jack!' she called after him in despair, but he ignored her. He passed Spiro making his way towards them, and spoke curtly to him, jerking his head in her direction.

Spiro glanced from Jack's face to Callie's slumped shoulders in surprise and began to say something, but Jack cut him off, gesturing impatiently with his hand. Someone was shouting and beckoning from one of the launches and Jack began to run towards it, either ignoring or not hearing whatever Spiro called after him, because he didn't turn round. He splashed through the water, the launch reversing even as he climbed on board.

It roared out to sea, leaving a foaming wake behind it and an unnatural silence on the beach. Two policemen were carefully transferring the box from the collapsed inflatable to the remaining launch, and only Callie and Spiro were left.

The night breeze lifted Callie's hair away from her face, and she could feel the sand beneath her feet, but she couldn't feel anything else. It was as if she were caught up in some ghastly nightmare, unable to move or cry out. Jack thought she was involved with Marcus. His words echoed like remembered blows. He had seen her holding the gun and the statue and in the confusion had drawn his own conclusions.

He had been very quick to think the worst, Callie thought desolately.

Spiro was talking to her. He looked worried, and seemed to be trying to tell her something, but Callie no longer cared. She was too tired to make an attempt to understand.

She touched his arm. '*Efharisto*, Spiro,' she said awkwardly. 'Thanks' seemed an inadequate word to thank someone for saving your life, and to apologise for so misjudging him, but it was the only word she knew.

Spiro looked at her tired face and seemed to understand that she wasn't capable of any more at present. He smiled and nodded before taking her arm and leading her gently down to the waiting launch.

They dropped her on the jetty below the villa, and because she had nowhere else to go Callie got out and smiled mechanically.

'*Efharisto,*' she said again, unable to think of anything else to say.

Beaming at her, they shouted their goodnights and roared off into the night, leaving her utterly alone in the darkness. It was only when they had gone that she realised that she still held the statue of the boy in her hand.

It was the first thing she saw the next morning when she awoke from a leaden sleep. For a moment she lay blinking at him, wondering what he was doing on her bedside table. His carved eyes stared serenely through her, not answering, and slowly the events of the night before began to filter back into her consciousness.

Jack's hard face, the unwinking eye of Marcus's gun, Spiro helping her into the boat: it all seemed unreal, and if it hadn't been for the calm, enigmatic face on her bedside table she would have thought it a bad dream.

Callie stared up at the ceiling and listened. The sea against the rocks, the whisper of leaves in the breeze, but otherwise silence. The villa felt echoingly empty without Jack.

He had said he was going to Athens. Did that mean he would be away long? And would he want to see her here when he came back?

Callie thought not. 'I don't care,' he had said. She had pushed him too far this time. There was no point in trying to explain. It didn't matter that he hadn't understood what she was doing on the beach. What mattered was what he thought, and he thought that she was stupid and gullible and deceitful. Callie's face tightened, but she wouldn't cry.

Instead she got up and dressed listlessly. She would have to leave the island before Jack returned. She should never have been here in the first place.

On the terrace, she calculated her money. She had spent hardly anything since she had been here and if she was careful she could spin it out for another three weeks. All she had to do was get herself to another island and carry on as she had originally intended. She could pretend that Garth Havelock's villa had never been mentioned, forget that she had ever come to Pikos and met Jack. She would forget the curl of his mouth and the smile that lurked in his eyes. She would forget how he had unravelled her senses and dared her to give herself up to the moment. She would forget the kiss on the jetty and the long, enchanted afternoon on the beach.

It was a forlorn hope. She knew she would never forget.

Her face looked gaunt in the mirror, her eyes huge and lost. An ugly bruise was spreading over her cheek. She looked terrible.

Callie sighed and reached for her hat. What did it matter what she looked like if Jack wasn't here? She walked down to the port, clutching her phrase book.

'When is the next ferry?' she asked Katerina in the taverna, reading the Greek translation haltingly from the book. She had to repeat it twice before Katerina realised what she was asking, and then there was the problem of understanding her reply. In the end Katerina took the phrase book from her and pointed to the answer.

'Thursday,' Callie read, following Katerina's finger. 'But that's another three days!'

Jack would be back long before then. She had to find some other way of getting off the island. She couldn't bear to face the dislike and distrust in his face again.

Callie wandered disconsolately out into the hot sunshine. Pikos looked just as it had done when she had arrived. There was even the same cat washing its ears on the quayside. The geraniums still stood on the dusty steps, the fishing boats still rocked gently in the breeze...boats! Callie stiffened. Surely she could pay one of the fishermen to take her to Ilonika?

Spiro was sitting outside the shop with several other men and she rushed over to him. There was a frustrating delay while she thumbed frantically through the phrase book for the right words. Spiro waited courteously, but when at last she managed a mangled question he simply shook his head with an air of finality.

'Oh, *please*! You must!' Callie went back to her book. Perhaps she'd got the wrong word.

She tried again, but Spiro was unmoved. He pointed up to the villa and seemed to be trying to tell her to go back, but Callie shook her head.

'You don't understand! I've got to go before Jack gets back.'

Spiro was clearly not going to help her, so she turned to the other men. One of them must be willing to earn some extra money, surely? She asked all of them until she was beginning to sound quite fluent, but they all shook their heads as Spiro had done.

Baffled, Callie gave up. She trudged back up the hill to the villa, wondering why they were all so obstinate. If Jack came back she would have to tell him that she had done her best to leave.

She sat miserably on the terrace, only to see a boat heading towards Ilonika. What was the betting it was Spiro? she thought bitterly. She was sure that he knew quite well what she wanted.

Expecting Jack back at any minute, Callie was tense and nervous, but when after two days he still hadn't arrived she began to think that he wouldn't come back at all until he was sure she had left, and somehow that was even worse. She threw herself into the illustrations and in her unhappiness drew some of her best work ever. The scenes she drew were clear and vivid, but invested with a tangible sense of enchantment so that the mythological figures leapt from the page like old, familiar faces, instantly recognisable.

By the time Thursday came Callie was calmer, but her heart was a cold stone of misery inside her. She packed her bags with a leaden sense of disaster and closed the door of the villa quickly behind her, desperate in case her control should break. She almost ran up the track without daring to look back at the villa clinging to the hillside, smothered in pink and purple swaths of bougainvillaea, nestled among the lemon trees and oleanders, the silver glint of the olive groves rippling in the wind around it and the intense blue of the sea beyond.

She was too early for the ferry. For want of anything better to do, she crossed the square again to the taverna and ordered a coffee. On an impulse she chose a chair at the table where she and Jack had sat the first time she had met him. If she closed her eyes she could imagine him as clearly as if he were still sitting opposite her, navy-blue eyes alight with reckless charm, every angle of his face engraved on her memory. The longing to see him was like a knife twisting in her heart.

Katerina was standing by the table with the cup of coffee, and Callie quickly opened her eyes, conscious that they were brimming with tears. Katerina gave her a wide smile and patted her shoulder comfortingly, pointing out into the bay with her hand. The ferry was just steaming round the headland and heading towards the harbour.

Perhaps she thinks I'm homesick, Callie thought, gazing dully at the ferry. It was getting closer by the second and she was suddenly overwhelmed with panic at the thought of leaving this lovely island and any hope of seeing Jack again behind.

But there was nothing for it but to drink her coffee and go. Leaving some money on the table, Callie picked up her bags and walked back to the quay. Her legs felt stiff and unnatural, as if she were sleep-walking. The men outside the shop nodded and smiled as she passed. Why were they so cheerful all of a sudden? she wondered, struggling against a wave of bitter, black despair.

With a triumphant blast of its horn the ferry docked against the quay and the waiting men leapt into action, pulling down the ramp to let the passengers off. Callie waited to one side as two women with huge baskets of vegetables got off, talking volubly, and then bent to pick up her bags.

'Going somewhere, Calypso?'

The bags slipped from her hands as she straightened in shock and incredulous joy.

'Jack!' Her grey eyes shone silver as she stared at him. He was looking very smart in grey trousers, white shirt and tie, but otherwise it was the same Jack, his hair ruffled by the sea breeze and the smile deepening the crease in his cheek.

Then she remembered the last time she had seen him, and the light went out of her eyes. 'I'm just going.'

'So I see,' said Jack, making no attempt to move out of her way. 'You're not running back to Neil, are you?'

'No,' said Callie sadly. 'I wouldn't go back to him before, and I won't now.'

'Where *are* you going, then?'

'I don't really know. Anywhere.' Callie couldn't look at him. 'I know you wanted me to leave straight away, but I had to wait for the ferry. I tried to get one of the fishermen to take me to Ilonika, but they wouldn't do it.'

'I know,' said Jack, taking her arm and turning her away from the ferry. 'I told Spiro to make sure you stayed on the island.'

Callie looked down at his hand, warm and strong against her skin, and then up into his face. 'But...I thought you'd never want to see me again!'

'I might have thought that for five murderous minutes the other night, but even then I told Spiro I wanted to deal with you myself. Have you had lunch?'

The abrupt change of subject caught Callie off balance. 'No, but——'

'Well, let's go and have some, then,' Jack said cheerfully. 'I'm starving.'

'I don't want to miss the ferry,' she muttered.

'Why not?'

'Oh, Jack, I've been such a fool about everything!' she burst out. 'About Marcus and about Garth Havelock and about you. I should go and let you get on with your life as it was before.'

Jack's hand tightened on her arm. 'The trouble is that I won't be able to do that. My life would never be the same now.'

'I won't tell a soul about your pseudonym, I promise!'

'I didn't mean that. I meant without you.'

One of the men was shouting from the ferry, obviously asking if Callie was coming or not, but they ignored him. Callie stood staring into Jack's eyes, hardly daring to believe what she read there, while a wild, impossible hope crept into her heart and a smile trembled on her lips.

The sailor shrugged, rolled his eyes and gave the order for the ramp to be pulled up.

Oblivious to it all, Jack took Callie into his arms and kissed her. It was a long, deep, sweet kiss as the ferry pulled away from the quay and the sailors leant over the rails and whistled at them.

When at last Jack raised his head the ferry was far out to sea and Callie's eyes were starry with happiness.

'I'll have to catch the next ferry now,' she teased.

'You won't be catching any ferry,' Jack said firmly, kissing her again. 'Now or ever. You're staying right here with me.' He laid his hand against her cheek. 'But first I need to explain why I was such a brute to you that night on the beach.'

'You probably want to know what I was doing there with a gun as well,' Callie said. 'I can imagine what you thought.'

'If I'd been less jealous of Marcus and furious with you for going off with him I might have stopped to think instead of jumping to the wrong conclusions. As soon as I'd had a chance to cool down, I realised that only an idiot would have thought you knew how to handle a gun, even if you hadn't been too transparently honest to have been involved in Marcus's shady dealings.'

Pulling her against him, Jack rested his cheek on her fine dark hair. 'I'm sorry, Calypso. I kept remembering your face as I walked away. You looked as if I'd hit you. I was as bad as Marcus.' He lifted her chin and traced the fading bruise on her cheekbone. 'Did he do this?'

Callie nodded and his arms tightened about her again. 'It's just as well I didn't know that when I was sitting in that boat with him.'

'It doesn't hurt any more,' she said. Nothing hurt any more, not with Jack's arms around her. 'What happened to them?'

'I'll tell you about it over lunch,' said Jack, taking her hand and leading her back to the square. 'Leave your bags here; we'll pick them up later. I was in such a hurry to get back in time to get the ferry that I missed breakfast this morning, and you don't look as if you've been eating properly either.'

Katerina rushed over to greet him, wreathed in smiles and chattering non-stop, and Jack glanced down at Callie.

'What's she saying?' she asked.

'She says she told you I was coming on the ferry, but she didn't think you understood. She says you looked as if your heart was breaking, but she knew everything would be all right as soon as you saw me.'

The warmth rose up in Callie's face, but she smiled at Katerina. 'Tell her she was right.'

They ordered souvlakia and a Greek salad, and Maria insisted on bringing them a bottle of her best retsina. With the bright sunlight dappling through the wicker shade and the wine glass chill in her hand, Callie looked across at Jack and felt happiness tighten her throat.

'Was your heart really breaking?' Jack asked quietly.

'Yes,' she said, and her heart was in her eyes as she smiled at him. 'I thought I was never going to see you again.'

'I would have come back sooner, but I was too pig-headed and angry to want to see you at first. Then Spiro rang me from Ilonika and said you were trying to leave. He also told me what really happened that night on the beach.'

He paused. 'I know now I was a complete fool—that's what Spiro said anyway! We'd left him to keep an eye on things outside while we went into the beach so the police could catch Marcus and his sidekick red-handed. Apparently he saw you coming down the cliff and at first he wasn't too sure what you were doing there either, but then you hid behind a rock, so at least he knew that Marcus wasn't expecting you. He watched you go down to the boat and let out the air, and was just silently congratulating you on a smart move when Marcus appeared. He didn't have any idea how long we were going to be, so he just tried to get close enough to hear what Marcus was saying. I gather he was afraid when you spotted him that you might give him away to Marcus, but he said you were wonderful, just kept very calm and diverted Marcus's attention just at the right moment.'

Reaching over, Jack took her hand and stroked her palm. 'That was brave of you, Calypso. You don't ever need to think of yourself as timid again.'

'I was terrified,' Callie said frankly, curling her fingers around his. 'And I owe Spiro a big apology as well as thanks.'

'Spiro? Why?'

'Well, I always thought Spiro looked so shifty,' she explained with some embarrassment. 'I was convinced he was up to no good, and you said he knew about the grotto, even though you were so insistent about keeping it a secret.'

Callie tucked her hair behind her ears and looked down into her wine. She didn't want to meet Jack's eyes, but her hand tightened around his. 'That night—after we had that quarrel—I saw lights on the beach from the terrace. It was silly to go on my own, but I had to know who it was. When I saw Philippe I was so relieved. You see, I thought . . . I thought it might have been you.'

'Me?' Jack sounded stunned.

'I know it sounds ridiculous, but remember how vague you were about what you were doing here,' Callie said, plucking up courage. 'I didn't know then that you were Garth Havelock. You had this image as a sort of layabout, but it didn't fit—now I know why! Anyway, I was a bit suspicious about you, and then I saw you and Spiro on the jetty one day. You didn't know I was watching. I didn't think anything about it at the time, but later, when we'd been to the grotto, I wondered what it was you'd been carrying so carefully, so I . . . I'm sorry, but I looked in your room and I found the statue in the chest.' Now that she had confessed she could look directly at him. 'I shouldn't have looked, I know.'

Jack sat back with a smile. 'So that was it! Why didn't you ask me about it, you silly girl?'

'I was going to, but then you said you would tell me everything that evening.' Callie's eyes dropped again, and she blushed. 'I thought you were going to confess to stealing pieces from the grotto to sell on the black market. Instead you invited Nikki to stay, and I was so jealous that I went off with Marcus and had an absolutely miserable time!'

'Poor Calypso!' grinned Jack. 'No wonder you were confused, but I'm glad you hated being with Marcus. If it's any comfort, I had an equally miserable time listening to Nikki yakking about chalet parties and all the jolly japes they get up to at their wretched barbecues. I only invited her as I thought she might have some idea what Marcus was up to, but the poor girl was clueless. I did manage to get some information about his movements, but the main thing was that she obviously went back and told him how interested I was in him. That must have decided him to get out while the going was good, but fortunately by then I'd taken your advice and informed the police, so we were able to organise a reception committee.'

'I still don't understand what the statue was doing in your room,' Callie complained.

'I'd better go back to the beginning.' Jack refilled her glass and then his own before setting the retsina bottle carefully back on the table. 'As Antonia told you, I'd planned to go to Los Angeles this summer, but I didn't *have* to be there, and just before I was due to leave Spiro came to see me. He said he'd been to the grotto and thought that a stranger had been there. It looked as if everything was still there, but some of the pieces had been moved, and he wasn't sure if anything was missing. I went along with him, and, sure enough, one of the statues had gone. I knew because there was a pair, and they were my favourite pieces.

'We talked about getting the police in, but we were still reluctant to let the authorities know about the grotto. Let's say Spiro wasn't too keen to have the police poking around Pikos! He'd never touch the grotto, but he does have a number of—er—sidelines that he'd prefer the police didn't find out about.'

Jack grinned at Callie. 'When you accused Spiro of being a suspicious-looking character you weren't that wide of the mark, but he's got a heart of gold, I promise you! Anyway, Spiro said he'd try and find out through his contacts if there was any sign of the statue on the black market. We managed to trace it to Athens, and I paid the dealer off. Spiro brought the statue back from Athens the day you saw us. I was going to put it back in the grotto, but I got rather diverted by the arrival of a lovely girl with big grey eyes . . . you. In fact, dearest Calypso, you made it very hard for me to concentrate on anything else!'

Katerina arrived at that moment, bearing plates laden with food. Callie had thought she wouldn't be hungry, but as soon as she smelt the lamb she found that she was ravenous.

'Did you really think I was involved with Marcus?' she asked a little later, when she had taken the edge off her hunger.

'Not really, no.' Jack shook his head and finished his mouthful. 'I was more jealous of him, especially when you kept telling me how nice he was! And you were so trusting that I was afraid he might try and use you somehow. I thought my worst dream had come true when I saw you on the beach holding that statue in one hand and a gun in the other, but I still couldn't face handing you over to the police with Marcus and Philippe.'

'What will happen to the grotto?' Callie asked, resting her elbows on the table. 'I suppose everyone knows about it now.'

'Perhaps it's for the best,' said Jack with a fatalistic shrug. 'It was always vulnerable for someone like Marcus to find. Pikos was lucky to keep its secret as long as it did. I asked the police chief to keep it quiet until I'd seen the minister of culture.'

'So that's what you were doing in Athens!'

'Fortunately he's a pal of mine—another fan!' Jack threw her one of his glinting smiles. 'But not as beautiful as you! He's agreed to keep the grotto closed to tourists, but obviously their archaeologists will have to have access.'

'At least the grotto will be safe,' Callie said comfortingly.

'I hope so. For a time, anyway.' He seemed to shake his doubts aside, and smiled at her. 'Shall we take the statues back this afternoon, while we can still have the grotto to ourselves?'

And so they walked back along the cliff-tops to the hidden bay with the scent of wild thyme drifting in the sunshine, just as it had done before. The bay lay quietly waiting for them, its clear turquoise waters still and calm.

Callie thought of her last headlong rush through the night, of those long minutes of fear on the beach, and she reached for Jack's hand. Together they made their way down to the sand and through the narrow crevice to the grotto.

It was as silent and serene as it had been before, in spite of the scuffle marks on the sand and the empty spaces where the other piece had lain undisturbed for so long. Now they were in some museum, being numbered and catalogued under harsh modern lighting.

Jack placed his statue behind the mosaic where it could look towards the sea, and Callie put hers carefully beside it. They were a perfectly matched pair, the boy staring through time and his friend turning to watch him, sharing the same timeless amusement.

'They belong together, don't they?' she said, and Jack nodded, smiling.

'Like us.'

Outside, the sea sparkled enticingly. Jack looked at it with a smile quirking his mouth and Callie knew that he was remembering how they had made love in the warm shallows. She smiled at him, the memory glowing in her eyes.

'Have you forgiven me for being Garth Havelock yet?' Jack said as they walked barefoot along the sand. 'It's such a damn-fool name, but I'm rather stuck with it now.'

'I've forgiven you, but I'm finding it harder to forgive myself for being so stupid about it.'

'I should have told you,' he admitted. 'Most of what I told you about him is true. I did go through a stage of being impressed with myself for being a successful writer, and after that I tried to keep the writer in me separate from the rest. In many ways I do feel that Garth Havelock is almost a separate character.'

Jack looked down into Callie's gentle, pointed face. 'Does it sound stupid if I say I was almost jealous of him when you turned him into such a hero? I wanted you to love me, Jack, not some image you'd created from reading my books. When you told me on the terrace that you'd come away with me if I asked, in spite of Garth, I felt...' He stopped and looked at the horizon, where blue sea blended into blue sky. 'Writing is my trade, but I can't find the words to describe how I felt, Calypso.

'I think I fell in love with you when you walked off that ferry with those silver eyes and that hint of something deeper and more passionate behind the shyness.' Smiling, he pushed the hair gently away from her face. 'My own personal nymph...do you love me too?'

'You know I do,' said Callie simply.

'I asked you once before if you'd like to be Mrs Garth Havelock—do you remember?—and you said no. Now that you know what you do, will you change your mind?'

'No.'

Taken aback, Jack repeated, 'No?'

'You were right about Garth, Jack. He was just an image I made up for myself. I don't want to marry a false image, but if you asked me to be Mrs Jack Kingsley I might give you a different answer.'

'Will you?' There was a warmth in his blue eyes that she had never seen before.

'Yes.'

Callie found herself swept into a kiss that left her breathless and quivering with the promise of love. Leaning back slightly against the circle of his arms, she smiled mischievously. They were standing on the shoreline, with the waves rippling over their feet.

'Shall we jump into deep water?'

'Who needs that kind of excitement?' said Jack, pulling her down on to the sand beside him. 'I seem to remember I rather liked it here last time. Let's stay in the shallows.'

HARLEQUIN ROMANCE®

A Halloween treat that's better than candy and almost as good as a kiss!

Two delightful frightful Romances from two of our most popular authors:

HAUNTED SPOUSE by Heather Allison
(Harlequin Romance 3284)
"Frizzy Lizzie" the Scream Queen confronts her handsome ex-husband—over a haunted house!

TO CATCH A GHOST by Day Leclaire
(Harlequin Romance 3285)
Zach Kingston wants to debunk Rachel Avery's family ghost. Rachel objects—and so does the ghost!

Available in October—just in time for Halloween!—wherever Harlequin books are sold.

HRHT

1993 Keepsake

CHRISTMAS

Stories

Capture the spirit and romance of Christmas with KEEPSAKE CHRISTMAS STORIES, a collection of three stories by favorite historical authors. The perfect Christmas gift!

Don't miss these heartwarming stories, available in November wherever Harlequin books are sold:

ONCE UPON A CHRISTMAS by Curtiss Ann Matlock
A FAIRYTALE SEASON by Marianne Willman
TIDINGS OF JOY by Victoria Pade

ADD A TOUCH OF ROMANCE TO YOUR HOLIDAY SEASON WITH KEEPSAKE CHRISTMAS STORIES!

HX93